LOYAL

Kay Jay Smith

HerJourney Publishing Company, Inc.

Houston, Texas

Kay Jay Smith

HerJourney Publishing Company, Inc.
Houston, TX 77267
Tel: 877-648-6597
hjpbooks@gmail.com

All HerJourney titles, imprints, and distributed lines are available at special quantity discounts for bulk purchases for sales promotion, premiums, fund raising, educational, or institutional use.

Special book excerpts or customized printings can also be created to fit specific needs. For details, write or phone the office of the HerJourney Sales Manager: Attn. Special Sales Department. HerJourney Publishing Co. Inc., Houston, TX 77267. Phone: 1-877-648-6597.

ISBN-10: 0-615-41469-9
ISBN-13: 978-0-615-41469-0

First Trade Paperback Printing: October 2010
Printed in the United States of America

Cover Art: Myrna Galan, Galan Graphics
Author photo: Jordan T. Smith

LOYAL

Thanking......

Giving all glory and honor to my Savior, **Jesus Christ**, for without Him there is no me.

My babies, **Jordan** and **Jacobi**, for putting up with me and loving me unconditionally. You are the reason I get up every morning. I love you more than life itself.

Lane, for being my friend when all else failed.

My parents, **David, Brenda** and **James**, who tried to raise me right and did a pretty good job.

My siblings, **Robbie, Christian, Christall, David, Bobby, Cheri, Jamie** and **Taylor**. Together, we are unstoppable. You make being the oldest a pleasure.

My nieces and nephews, **Kiana, Willie, Sapphire, Mikkell, Christopher, Ahriel, Zamir, King David, David IV** and **Sir Genius (Geno)**. Each and every one of you is special in your own unique way. Treasure that.

My best friends, **Kimberly, Mario, James, Shann, Stephanie** and **Alice**. You all have my back in some extraordinary ways. I appreciate you.

My friend, **Loranda Manney, Entrusted Business Networks**, for taking the reins when I get stuck.

Gremillion & Pou and Associates, Shreveport, LA.

Xavier University, New Orleans, LA.

Delgado Community College, New Orleans, LA.

St. Augustine's Church, New Orleans, LA.

The Louisiana Superdome, New Orleans, LA.

Bourbon Orleans Hotel, New Orleans, LA.

New Orleans House of Blues and **Live Nation.**

Hilton Hotels and **Hilton Americas** - Houston, TX.

InterContinental Hotels Group and **Holiday Inn Downtown** Shreveport, LA.

The Cheesecake Factory, Inc. and **Grand Lux Café**, Houston, TX.

The Woodlands Mall, The Woodlands, TX.

Rockfish Seafood Grill, The Woodlands, TX.

Isiah Carey and **Fox 26 News**, Houston, TX.

George R. Brown Convention Center, Houston, TX.

Willowbrook Methodist Hospital, Houston, TX.

To all the family, friends and businesses not mentioned, you are deeply appreciated.

My friend, **Terri**. You are loved and missed. This one's for you, 'Lucy'.♥

PREFACE

I hope you enjoy reading this book as much as I enjoyed writing it. There was laughter, tears, joy and sorrow while writing LOYAL. I didn't expect to sell it nor have people love it as much as I do.

Hopefully, this book will allow a woman to see how it should feel to be pursued by a man that really sees her worth. A woman's worth is set by the woman. It is our job as women to let our worth shine and be known.

Men, let this be a guide as to how women want to be and should be treated.

♥ Kay Jay

Kay Jay Smith

LOYAL

Kay Jay Smith

LOYAL

CHAPTER 1

Eli Johnson came into the house and tossed his cognac colored leather briefcase on the dining room table. Naomi, his wife, was standing at the stove stirring a pot of red beans she was cooking for dinner. She was startled as Eli came in.

"Baby, what's wrong?" Naomi asked as she tapped her spoon on the side of the pot and put the lid on.

She wiped her hands on her red and white gingham apron and walked over to her husband who had taken a seat at the table. He looked as though he had the weight of the world on his shoulders.

"No one is hiring engineers here in Houston, Naomi! All the work is coming out of Louisiana right now," he said as he removed his blue silk necktie. "You wouldn't believe how many doors were closed in my face today. I have all this experience and no one wants it!"

He slammed his big fist on the table. Naomi stood behind her man and wrapped her arms around his broad shoulders. She could feel the tension in those shoulders. He came home this way many times before in the past few weeks.

Eli and Naomi Johnson had been married for 20 years and as long as she had known him he worked and took care of her and their 16 year old twin sons, Marlon and Leon. He never knew what it was to be unemployed until that fateful day when the company he worked for laid him off after 19 years of service.

Now, here he was looking for a job and trying to make ends meet. They had his unemployment checks and savings in the bank, but it was going fast. The boys were trying to do their share by doing little odd end jobs, but it just wasn't enough.

"Maybe I should get a job," Naomi said quietly looking at the top of his graying head. She knew how Eli felt about this subject.

They both agreed that she would take care of the boys and their home and he would go out and work.

LOYAL

"Naomi, that isn't even an option and you know it," Eli said as he pulled her onto his lap. "You are the backbone of this household and with your leg acting up that would only cause more problems."

She kissed him on his forehead and cheeks then gently on his lips. This was a little ritual they started years ago. As she looked deep into his light brown eyes she thought about how she'd loved this man every since she could remember. She thought she probably loved him before she even met him.

"I need to really pray about this situation," Eli said as they both got up from the chair.

He patted her on her bottom and she swatted him with her dish towel.

"Your dinner will be ready in a few minutes," she said with a warm smile.

Eli went upstairs and passed by each of his boy's rooms. He looked at the trophies and the posters on the walls.

He remembered how they used to play ball in the park and ride bikes. The boys were growing up by leaps and bounds now. They had dates and jobs and Leon even sported a slight mustache. He smiled as he went into the bathroom to run some bath water. A hot bath always helped him think. As he stepped into the steaming tub he looked up and asked God what he should do. That is when he heard it as clear as if God were standing right there in the bathroom with him.

"*Move to New Orleans,*" Eli was stunned and very still.

He closed his eyes and prayed.

"Lord, if I heard what I heard correctly can you please confirm it with a sign? I don't want to pack my family up and disrupt their lives because I thought I heard something."

The room was quiet except for drops of water from the faucet into the steaming tub. Eli finished his bath and went down to have dinner with his family. The boys had come in from their after school activities and were full of things to talk about.

"Hey, Pop!" Marlon said as his father approached the table.

"Hey, son! How was practice today?" Eli loved to hear the boys talk about their sports. It reminded him of when he was in school scoring all the points.

LOYAL

"Aw man, he didn't do nothing interesting today because I was running circles around him!" Leon, the oldest twin, joked from across the table.

Before Marlon could jump in to defend himself, Naomi interrupted, "Um, excuse me sir, but *didn't do nothing?*"

"I mean...uh, he didn't do *anything* interesting today," Leon stammered.

"Thank you, sir," Naomi said, as she smoothed his hair with her hands.

After Naomi put the fried chicken, corn on the cob, collard greens, red beans and rice on the table, she stood next to Eli's chair and said,

"Maybe we should move to Louisiana. If that's where the jobs are, that is where we should be."

Eli just shook his head, smiled and blessed the table.

CHAPTER 2

Settling into New Orleans was a big adjustment for everyone. The people were friendly, but it just wasn't home. Houston and New Orleans were like night and day! New Orleans seemed to never sleep. Everywhere you turned, you heard music playing and people having a good time. There were lots of enticing things for two teenage boys, also.

It was hard for them to adjust to their new high school because everyone knew they were from Texas. The guys saw them as competition and the girls just liked having someone different around. This made for plenty of confrontations in and out of school. Eventually the newness wore off and the boys became known as "the twins". Both boys excelled in school. They buried themselves in their studies and sports. They barely had time to breathe. By the time graduation came two years later, the boys were ready for whatever college had to offer them.

It was around this time that Eli became very ill. He barely made it to the boys' graduation ceremony. Eli was a stubborn man and rarely went to the doctor. He was always having Naomi make up a batch of this or that to cure him of his ailments. Naomi begged him to go the doctor, but he would always say, "Why should I give someone good money to tell me to take two aspirin and call them in the morning?" Naomi was worried, but what could she do.

The last straw was when Eli got up to go into the kitchen for something to drink one evening. As he walked, his head started swimming like he was under water. He felt a sharp pain in his head. He could hear Naomi call his name, but when he turned to face her he fell backward and hit his head. Naomi screamed and ran over to him as Marlon dialed 911. The boys carried their fragile looking father to the couch where he laid until the ambulance reached them.

At the hospital, the doctor explained that Eli had a massive stroke and how he'd overworked his heart and body. The stress from the job and his poor diet had taken its toll on his 49 year old body.

Naomi was devastated. She had never seen Eli look so helpless. She rarely left his side the whole two weeks he was in ICU.

Marlon and Leon kept the house together for her while she was with Eli. There was nothing else to do, but wait and pray. While their father was in the hospital, the twins began to talk about their futures.

"We can't just leave Mama here with Pop the way he is and it's almost time to start school in the fall," Marlon said.

"Don't you think I've been thinking about this, too?" Leon spat, with his muscular jaw set just like his father's when he was in deep thought.

"We have to go to college, but maybe we can just go around here until Pop gets better so we can help Mama out."

Both of the boys planned to go back to Texas for their college education. There was no way they could leave now. Not with how things were. The boys prayed that God would show them the answers.

One evening the phone rang. It was their mother. She told the boys that they should come down to the hospital as fast as possible and to be careful. As they sped to the hospital there was complete silence in the car. You could tell both of them were praying from the movement of their lips. Marlon parked the car and they ran through the hospital corridors to their father's room. Naomi was lying across Eli's body, wailing uncontrollably. Leon dropped to his knees at the door and Marlon ran over to his mother and held her tightly. Eli Johnson was dead.

The doctor came in and explained that while Eli was sleeping he suffered another stroke. This one was fatal.

Naomi steadied herself on her own two feet. She leaned over and gently kissed Eli's forehead, cheeks and then gently on his lips.

Marlon and Leon helped their mother out of the room and down the hallway to the elevator. As they waited, Naomi screamed, *"Why God?!"*

The elevator bell chimed and the doors opened.

CHAPTER 3

After Eli's death, Naomi's life was a sad routine. Get up in the morning. Cry. Fix breakfast for the boys before their college classes. Cry. Clean the already clean house. Cry. Take a call or two from friends who checked in on her from time to time. Cry. Cook dinner. Cry. Go to bed. Cry. She couldn't stop crying.

She had lost her best friend in the whole world. The only person who knew her like a book. Her lover and her confidante. There would be no replacing Eli. She vowed to herself that she would never try. What was the use? No one could ever fill his shoes.

Even in death, Eli was still taking care of his family. A $750,000 insurance policy he and Naomi purchased for each other years ago paid off the houses in New Orleans and Houston along with the cars. Naomi didn't have to work.

LOYAL

Meanwhile, Marlon and Leon were trying to carry on as best as possible. They got special permission from the dean to live off campus with their mother due to her fragile state. Someone had to take care of her. They really missed their father. No one to shoot the breeze with or discuss the latest female admirers with. Leon would catch his mother staring at him because he looked so much like his father. This made him feel both sad and proud at the same time.

Naomi encouraged the boys to have lives outside of the house and school. She often told them that they babied her too much. She also reminded them that she was never going to get grandchildren if they sat in the house looking at her all the time.

For the next two years things were run by routine in their household. Finally, Naomi had enough.

"I want you two out of my house tonight and do not come back until you've had some fun."

Looking at each other like their mother had just lost her mind, they laughed as they got ready for the evening.

What could two strapping 20 year old bachelors get into on Saturday night in the Big Easy? They decided to hit the House of Blues on Decatur Street. Good food, good music and good looking women. You couldn't beat that.

"Wow! We haven't been out in a minute!" Marlon said, as they walked down the sidewalk.

"I know. Since Pop died I really haven't been in the mood, but the music is jumpin' in here!" Leon said, snapping his fingers to the beat.

When they got inside they each took a different side of the room. They played this game since they were children. Find an unsuspecting soul and take turns talking to her until she realized something like the mole by Marlon's left eye or that the guys were wearing two totally different outfits. It broke the ice and the monotony.

This night wasn't going to be an exception until the brothers noticed almost at the exact same time two young ladies sitting in a booth. The twin radar went off and they slid into the booth next to the ladies. They introduced themselves and after a few corny jokes and some good food they all felt like they had known each other for years.

LOYAL

Marlon and Leon decided that Ruth and Opal, O for short, were two of a kind. They wanted to see each other again. Phone numbers were exchanged and they went their separate ways.

Several phone calls and dinners later, they all discovered that they had attended rival high schools where Ruth and Opal had been cheerleaders. The couples went everywhere and did everything together. They became inseparable.

Naomi sat back and watched her young men blossom with these young ladies. Naomi liked them. She felt very comfortable and the girls even took to calling her 'Mama Naomi'. It had been 2 ½ years since Eli passed and her house was finally filling with life. She enjoyed cooking for her family again. She enjoyed the laughter in the house. She was starting to feel content once more.

That is when the boys came to her one day after being out with Ruth and O.

"Mama, we need your opinion on something," Marlon said.

"Ok, but you know I am going to give it to you straight." Naomi laughed because she had picked up a nasty little habit of 'giving it to you straight' since Eli had been gone.

"Ma, we think we want to marry Ruth and O," Leon said with a very serious look on his face.

They didn't know if Naomi would think that it was too soon. They desperately wanted her approval.

"Well," she started. "Ruth and O are like daughters I never had," she paused and looked at both of them.

They had such serious looks on their faces. She was laughing on the inside because she had been waiting for this moment for a while. "But I don't know if I would want to marry a young man who *thinks* he wants to marry me!"

Naomi was laughing now. Her sons looked at her as she laughed so hard tears came to her eyes. She walked toward them and hugged her big, tall, strong sons. It seemed just like yesterday that they were playing around her skirt hem and now she had to reach up on her tip toes to get around their necks. They picked her up and swung her around. Now they were all laughing and crying. Crying tears of joy.

Ruth Marie Thibodaux was a quiet girl. She wasn't like most of the girls she'd gone to high school with. She excelled in her classes and she had been the captain of the cheerleading squad. By most people's standards, she was very pretty, but she didn't think so. Her light Creole skin and blue-green eyes made some of the other girls very jealous of her.

All the guys in school tried to date her at least once during high school, but she would politely turn them down and keep walking. She had no time for the foolish games teenagers played in school. She had one goal in mind and that was going to college.

All her life her grandmother told her that education was the key to everything she wanted to do in life and education is what she planned on using to open every door.

She knew that she didn't want to end up like her mother, Marie. Ruth loved her mother, but she knew the road her mother took would not be her own. When Ruth was six years old her mother left her at her grandmother's house to run some errands. That was the last time she ever lived with her mother. The streets, the drugs and the men were her mother's weakness. Marie didn't even know who Ruth's father was. Grand-mère, which is Creole for grandmother, always argued with her daughter to take better care of her Ruth.

Kay Jay Smith

"One of these days, cher, I will take that baby away from you if you can't sit still with her! No child deserves to be dragged from place to place. They will never feel safe."

Marie would always argue back. "Mama, you can't tell me what to do! I am a grown woman and this is mon petit! MY BE'BE'!"

Out of all of the fighting and arguing Grand-mère and Marie did they would always come together when it concerned Ruth. Marie knew she could count on her mother when times got hard for her and her child.

Ruth grew up understanding that she had to love her mother, but she also needed to keep her distance emotionally from her.

"Hello, mon petit, this is your mama. Do you have any money you can loan me until I get my check?" Marie purred over the phone.

Marie was always asking her for money and Ruth used to give it to her. Ruth would give her mother her lunch money, church money and any money she could find. She just wanted her mother to get better. When Grand-mère found out she scolded both of them.

"You don't take anything from this child ever again! Do you hear me, Marie! And as for you, my Ruth, you don't give away anything

LOYAL

I give you! Do *you* hear me? People will use you and abuse you. It is up to you to stop them!"

At that moment, Ruth learned two valuable lessons. #1 was never to give anything away that Grand-mère gave her and #2 was to never let anyone get over on her, not even her own mother.

CHAPTER 4

Graduation seemed like it would never come, but for Ruth and her best friend, O, things couldn't get any better.

O was Ruth's best friend since the 9th grade. O even beat up a few girls for Ruth because they picked with Ruth so much. O wasn't as pretty as Ruth, but what she lacked in looks she surely made up for in personality. She and Ruth always had fun. Whenever one of them was down the other always found a way to bring her up. They did everything together. They even got their ears pierced together.

Ruth and O were like the sisters each of them never had. O appreciated the fact that even though Ruth had more advantages than she and even a little smarter she never rubbed it in.

O also had a rough life, but she didn't have a Grand-mère to save her. O lived with her mother and three brothers. The little shotgun house they lived in really should have held two people, but they made it work. Room was short and money was even shorter.

Being the only girl out of three boys was no walk in the park either. If they weren't fighting her, they were fighting her boyfriends. The only person they didn't harass was Ruth. That was only because they were all in love with her. They would fight over who she would sit by when she came to O's house.

"You need to raise up off my woman, Willie!" the youngest brother, Christopher said.

"Yo' woman?" screeched Mikkell, the middle boy.

"You heard me!" yelled Christopher, forgetting all about the Billy Dee voice he'd been using since Ruth walked in the door.

"All three of y'all are stupid and get away from my friend! You are drooling on her clothes!" O said as she started swatting her brothers with a pillow from the tattered couch.

They would even show off by talking about each other's mama while playing the dozens even though they all had the same mother. They could have easily talked about each other's fathers since they all had different ones. Even O had a different father.

Father's Day was interesting at the Broussard house. Four different cars pulling up one right after the other to come and collect their respective children. The neighbors had a field day with that one. Rachelle Broussard stood on her porch and kissed each one of her children goodbye and rolled her eyes at her nosy neighbors. Who did they think they were anyway? Judging her like that when she knew where most of them had been or where they were going when the street lights came on.

Rachelle liked Ruth. She liked the way her house seemed to change and everyone was on their best behavior when she came. Ruth liked Rachelle, too. She liked the fact that a mother actually took care of her children.

Ruth often longed to have her own mother come and take care of her that exact same way for many years until she realized that it wasn't going to happen.

After graduation, the girls decided to go to the local community college. After two years they would transfer to a bigger school. Actually, Ruth could have gone to any school she wanted. She didn't want to leave her friend behind. Needless to say, Grand-mère wasn't very happy about Ruth's choice, but she respected the loyalty she had to her friend.

"Cher, if this is what you want to do then do it. As long as you are in someone's school, I cannot complain."

That is why Ruth loved her grandmother and that is why O loved Ruth.

The two were well into their first semester of their second year when they met Marlon and Leon. They reminisced about the way the twins smoothly invited themselves to their table at the House of Blues. They laughed at the twins' corny jokes and even danced with them to the hip blend of jazz and R&B.

Ruth was instantly drawn to Leon. It was something about the way he talked and stared directly into her eyes. It was if he could see right through her. Many times throughout the evening the two of them forgot that Marlon and O were even there. When they went out onto the dance floor to dance to Etta James' *At Last*, she prayed the night would never end. To her, that would always be 'their' song.

Marlon and O hit it off as well. Marlon spent most of the night making O laugh, which was her favorite thing to do.

He was intrigued by her knowledge of all the sports that he liked and how she could hang with his conversation. In his mind, he had met his match, but he could never let her know that so soon. Little did he know that O felt the same way.

They would all just play it cool for now.

The couples saw more and more of each other. They had been dating for six months when Marlon and Leon proposed to the girls. They went to the beautiful Bombay Club on Conti Street in the French Quarters. The music was playing as they sat at a candlelit table watching the musicians do their thing. Both of the young men seemed nervous and the ladies were well aware of it.

"What is wrong with y'all?" O questioned while elbowing Ruth.

"Yeah, y'all are acting really funny, cher," Ruth chimed in.

Leon was wiping sweat from his forehead and Marlon kept fidgeting with his pocket. The guys looked at each other and nodded. They both hit one knee on opposite sides of the table in front of their girlfriends.

Ruth and O's eyes got big and everyone around them turned in their seats to see what was going on. Both of the women started crying as the guys pulled out light blue boxes with white ribbons from their pockets.

When Marlon and Leon opened the boxes the whole room fell silent. The music stopped and it was as if everyone was holding their breath waiting for Ruth and O to answer!

As they turned to look at each other, they smiled, looked at their future husbands and screamed, "YES, INDEED!!" The music started and the whole room erupted into laughter and clapping. Just then they saw Naomi coming out of the kitchen of the restaurant toward their table. They grabbed her and made one big hugging circle in the middle of the floor. Everyone was crying tears of joy! It just felt right.

CHAPTER 5

The wedding plans went on without a hitch. Of course, both weddings would be held together. One big wedding and one big party afterward would leave all of New Orleans talking for years to come. The ceremony would be held at St. Augustine Church and the reception would be held at the Bourbon Orleans. The date was set for Christmas day 2004 since the wedding was such short notice and all of the families would be together anyway.

A winter wedding in New Orleans. The colors of ebony, crimson and snow white were everywhere. The brides had their dresses especially made for them. They had a total of seven bridesmaids and seven groomsmen. There were three flower girls and one ring bearer. The church was decorated with every kind of red flower known to man. Candles glowed like twinkling stars in the dimly lit church as music played softly in the background. Friends and family had come from all over to see this once in a lifetime moment. The church was packed.

Naomi stayed in the room with her boys while they got ready. Since Eli wasn't there to help them, she felt it was her duty. They teased her about seeing them in their underwear. She blushed and tended to their tuxedos.

Secretly, she felt relieved that Marlon and Leon were getting married. She didn't like feeling like she was holding them back from life because she was alone. She also felt that it made it easier for her if she ever decided to go home to Texas.

She wouldn't be worried about whether or not they were eating and being taken care of like all good mothers do. She loved Ruth and O. She knew that they would do well by her sons. Naomi went over to her purse and pulled two boxes out. She called both of her sons over to the couch she was sitting on. When Naomi opened the boxes there were two beautiful gold bands. As she handed each of her sons a box she explained how she had taken hers and Eli's wedding rings and had them melted down and made into rings for each of them. She said that she always wanted them to have a part of her and Eli with them at all times. The tears flowed as both of the young men placed their rings on their right hands. They hugged their mother and laughed at how they were crying like little babies. Naomi left them to have a moment alone with each other and went down the hall to the bridal room.

There was Ruth. She was simply beautiful. Ruth's gown was a long white off the shoulder gown that showcased her beautiful face and hair. She glowed. Her curls cascaded down onto her shoulders. On her long slender neck she wore a strand of her grandmother's pearls. Her train flowed behind her as she paced back and forth. The makeup artist was trying to keep up with her even though she really didn't need any makeup.

Her grandmother was fussing and telling her to keep still as she tried to adjust the laces on the back of the dress. Her mother was nowhere to be found.

"Where is she, Grand-mère?" Ruth asked. "She promised she would be here!" Everyone in the room knew Ruth was talking about her mother, Marie.

"Cher, today is your day and you are not going to ruin it with talk of your mama!"

Grand-mère held Ruth by the shoulders as she stopped her to look in her eyes.

"You have a church full of loved ones out there waiting to see you and you are worried about one person? Leave it in God's hands, mon ami."

Just then Ruth turned to see Naomi standing in the doorway.

"I'm sorry, Ruth, I was just coming to see if you needed anything, baby. I'll come back later."

"No! Mama Naomi, you stay," Ruth said so abruptly that everyone stopped what they were doing. "I want you here, I need you here!" Ruth ran over to Naomi and buried her head in her shoulder.

"You are my mother now," Ruth whispered in her ear.

Naomi hugged Ruth with all the love she had in her heart at that moment.

"And you are my daughter now," Naomi whispered back.

They walked into the adjoining room where O was getting her last minute things together.

"You look marvelous, dah'link!" Ruth and O said in unison. They did that a lot.

"Thank you, dah'link!" They said in unison again.

"Mama Naomi, you look good, too!" O said as she and Ruth finished hugging.

O's mother, Rachelle, was busy fussing with O's hair, with bobby pins hanging out of her mouth.

"Cher, if you don't sit down I know something!" she said.

"Yes, ma'am!" O laughed.

Just then someone was knocking on the door calling for all of the bridesmaids, mothers and flower girls to line up. This sent everyone into a tizzy. Last minute hair sprays and lipstick fixes and everyone was out the door. Everyone except Ruth and O. They were left there to their own nerves.

"Girl, we can do this," Ruth said. "We've done everything else together so what makes this any different?"

Ruth squeezed O's hand as they walked down the aisle together. The flower girls had just finished blanketing the floor with red and white rose petals. Kiana, one of the flower girls, threw a handful of petals at her brother who was making faces at her as she went down the aisle.

LOYAL

The song that played was Ave Maria. This song reminded Ruth of her mother, but right before a tear could well up she caught a glimpse of Leon. He was so handsome. He looked even taller than usual. Marlon was handsome too, but there was something about Leon.

Even though he and Marlon were identical she could always tell the difference immediately. He was so sure of himself. He knew what he wanted in life and right now he wanted her. She was so in love with him. She couldn't wait to say her vows. She couldn't wait to say I do. She had dreamed of this day for as long as she could remember.

It seemed like they would never get to the end of the isle. Cameras were flashing and people were oooing and ahhing. It was all surreal. She closed her eyes and breathed in deeply. She wanted to remember this day for the rest of her life.

"I do!" "I do!" "I do!" and "I do!"

They rode in a white carriage with crimson velvet interior to the hotel for the reception after pictures. The carriage was pulled by two of the biggest coal black horses Ruth had ever seen. The weather was crisp and cool, but the ladies were wrapped in white mink wraps and muffs that Grand-mère gave them as wedding presents. When the carriage pulled up to the Bourbon Orleans they were greeted by guest dancing and waving white handkerchiefs and parasols.

The live jazz band was playing second line and led the crowd through the hotel foyer to the reception hall. Visitors in the lobby stopped and looked in awe as the wedding procession danced down the hallway. Everyone was smiling and laughing. Ruth thought that this was definitely the best day of her life. Nothing could ever top this.

They partied well into the morning. Party revelers still danced as they went out the door. Marlon, O, Leon and Ruth shook the last person's hand as they made their way toward their honeymoon suites. As they got on the elevator, they laughed at how O's drunk uncle, Pierre, had tried to hit on every woman in the party and how Marlon and Leon's cousin from Houston, Ariel, tried to show everyone how to do a cowboy two-step which might have worked if she hadn't kept forgetting the steps.

As they got off the elevator on their floor they all hugged and went their separate ways to bring in the new day as Mr. and Mrs. Johnson.

CHAPTER 6

The next few months passed like a blur. Ruth and O had just finished their two years at Delgado Community College and were going to Xavier University in the fall. Marlon and Leon were already at Xavier. They moved into off campus housing not far from Naomi. At least one of them popped in daily to see her and make sure she didn't need anything.

At fifty-two, Naomi was still young enough to get around town with her friends and try new things. She was even starting to think about Eli without having a breakdown.

Naomi was still not interested in dating, though. Her friends constantly had someone in mind for her, but she always said the same thing. "No one could fill these shoes" and she meant that.

Marlon and Leon, now twenty-one, were very big on community activities for the youth. They were constantly playing ball with the kids at the local community center or taking them to games. They felt they were giving back what their father had given them. They both eventually wanted children, but they wanted to finish their education first. They always joked about whose junior would beat who at different sports. They also knew that their mother was looking forward to grandchildren, but she understood that her boys wanted to have all their ducks in a row before bringing another life into this world. That didn't stop her from bringing it up every now and again at Sunday dinner.

The start of fall semester at Xavier was very different from Delgado, but the girls fell right in like they were naturals. Ruth loved meeting up with Leon in the middle of the big X for an afternoon kiss. That was one of the highlights of her day. She saw how the other girls looked at him, but she wasn't worried because she knew he was all hers.

August 29th, 2005 would forever be stained in Ruth's mind. That was the day that her life was turned upside down.

For most of the week, the newscasters had talked about a hurricane coming out of the Atlantic. The Johnson family was no stranger to hurricanes. They had weathered many storms in both

LOYAL

Louisiana and Texas, but this hurricane was slightly different from other storms that had pounded the Gulf Coast. It had already done major damage in Florida and was heading straight toward Louisiana and Texas.

The family got together to see what should be done. They heard talk of mandatory evacuation, but decided that they could weather the storm rather than get trapped on I-10 headed to Mississippi or Texas. Naomi's home was a two story made of brick; it was one of the only brick homes in the neighborhood. It also sat on a slight hill so the house was elevated. They felt safe. The house was full of grocery, all the cell phones were charged and the cars were full of gas just in case they needed to get out quick.

At 5 a.m. that day, Marlon's cell phone rang. It was, Simeon, one of the neighborhood kids they mentored saying he and his little sister were home alone and didn't know where their mother was. Simeon told Marlon that his mother had left in the middle of the night with her boyfriend and said that she would be right back. She never showed up. Marlon could hear the little sister crying in the background.

Marlon told the little boy to calm down and that he would be right over to get them. They only lived a few blocks from Naomi's house.

It was storming outside and the winds were blowing so hard that the trees were bending. O begged Marlon not to go. Leon said he would go with him to make sure everything was ok. Ruth knew there would be no changing her husband's mind. They all knew that two children left alone in weather like this was a deadly situation. As the men suited up to go out into the storm, Naomi prayed.

She pleaded the blood of Jesus over her sons, the children they were going to rescue and the mother who'd left them. All of the women were weeping which was very unnerving, but everyone agreed this had to be done.

They pulled Leon's SUV out of the garage and proceeded slowly down the street. It was raining so hard the rain was blowing sideways.

As the brake lights slowly disappeared down the street, Ruth struggled to close the garage door. She had a very bad feeling. After an hour of not being able to get through on the telephone, Ruth's cell phone rang. It was Leon. The connection was bad and all she heard was "…..have the children" and "….way back". Then the phone went dead. Ruth got another sinking feeling. She couldn't shake it. She tried to keep Naomi and O calm by making small talk, but they couldn't concentrate because of their crying.

Ruth's mind went to her Grand-mère who now resided at a nearby nursing home. The staff assured Ruth that everything was ok there and not to worry.

"Cher, I've seen plenty of storms in my day and not one of them have taken me out of here yet!" Grand-mere laughed as she and Ruth hugged.

"Ok, woman," Ruth joked. "I don't want to see you on the
news holding on to a stop sign!"

This woman had shown her so much love in her life. Being in Grand-mère's big arms was like home. Ruth couldn't even begin to think of her mother, Marie. She hadn't seen her since she ran into her outside of Rouse's Supermarket a few weeks after her wedding. She grabbed Ruth's left hand, looked at her ring and walked away. She didn't say hello or goodbye.

At that moment, Ruth knew she no longer had a mother.

Just as she was coming to the end of her daydream the lights flickered and went out. The women grabbed the flashlights and set out to light the candles they had strategically placed around the house. Just in case water made its way into the house from the street they started moving things up stairs. The women sang songs to keep themselves occupied and took turns trying Marlon and Leon's cell phones. By this time the lines were down. There was no calling in or out.

Looking very closely at her watch by candlelight, Ruth saw that it was 8:45 a.m., but it was pitch black outside. As the eye of the storm came nearer the women could hear trees cracking and debris hitting the house. Thank God the men had boarded up the windows with the wood Naomi kept in the garage. The women huddled together in a closet downstairs until Naomi felt water where she was sitting. As O turned on the flashlight they saw that waves of water were lapping under the door.

When Ruth opened the door a flood of water came rushing in. The women screamed and grabbed what they could keep from getting wet. They headed upstairs to the bathroom which was in the center of the house. This was a dangerous spot to be, but they had no choice with water climbing as rapidly as it was.

Naomi prayed out loud. *"Lord Jesus, please put your precious wings over this house and my boys."*

Just then there was a loud crashing sound and the house trembled. They couldn't be sure, but it sounded like it came from right outside the door. No one dared to move. They couldn't even if they wanted to. For what seemed like an eternity the rains and wind pounded the house. Then there was quiet. An eerie quiet. Again, no one moved.

After about thirty minutes of quiet the women came out of their crouching positions on the floor. It felt like they'd been there for hours.

In all of the excitement no one had notice the soaked floor they were sitting on. When they opened the door to the bathroom they couldn't believe their eyes. Half of the roof and the walls were missing! They were looking directly outside. As they cautiously moved around the unstable structure they began to cry. From the missing wall in the bedroom they saw the devastation. There was water everywhere. Water covered everything. Trees, houses and cars. Everything was gone.

The women looked toward the area Marlon and Leon were headed. It and everything as far as the eye could see was covered with water. Some rooftops of other homes were showing and people were starting to break through them with whatever they could. There was a woman screaming for someone to come help her mother who was stuck in the attic of her house. Men from another rooftop jumped into the murky water and tried to swim over to the now hysterical woman.

The water was carrying them away from the direction they were trying to go and they grabbed on to the nearest tree they could find. Others fashioned a makeshift rope from the debris passing by and made their way to the screaming woman.

No one could speak. The devastation was something out of a movie. Ruth and O tried to comfort Naomi as she started yelling Marlon and Leon's names. *"Not again, Lord, not my babies!"* she screamed at the top of her lungs.

The sinking feeling that Ruth had in the pit of her stomach would not leave. She felt like she wanted to vomit, but she knew she had to be strong for O and Naomi. The three women just stood there and watched as neighbor after neighbor broke through the roofs of their homes. There were crying children and women. Animals were treading water or clinging desperately to floating debris. People with aluminum fishing boats were riding from house to house taking people to dry land.

News helicopters were starting to fly around. The wind from the propellers was kicking up the water and people began to yell for them to go away for fear they would do more damage. It was a nightmare. Something no one ever expected in a million years. The two men trapped in the tree were finally rescued by a passerby in a boat.

One by one everyone who survived the storm on Naomi's street was rescued and taken to the Superdome.

As they rode to the Superdome they passed Grand-mere's nursing home. They saw that the water was to the top of the building. Ruth quickly turned her head and threw up over the side of the boat.

CHAPTER 7

At the Superdome, the women witnessed some of the saddest sights they had ever seen. Orphaned children and sick, elderly people just to name a few. Not to mention the crime and filth that lurked in every corner. The smell was horrendous. Everyone was angry.

News crews came in and interviewed people inside and outside of the Superdome. There were calls for President Bush to be impeached for the conditions people were living in. Babies had nothing to eat. The heat was making people drop like flies. New Orleans was like looking at a third world country. People were angry, hot, hungry and thirsty which led to many fights.

There were even stories of vigilante law enforcement killing innocent people.

LOYAL

On August 31st as Ruth, Naomi and O sat outside the Superdome they heard a woman speaking in an angry voice to a cameraman. When they stood up to see what all the commotion was about, it was O's mother, Rachelle. Right there on camera, they all had a reunion with tears and screams of joy and pain. The news crew got it all on camera along with the women's story of Marlon and Leon leaving to rescue the abandoned children. Rachelle told how she and her three sons had gotten to safety just as the levies collapsed and how they prayed that O and Ruth were safe. Rachelle tried to comfort her daughter by telling her that Marlon and Leon were probably somewhere safe, waiting for the water to go down.

On September 3rd, buses were being loaded to transport people out of the city. As the women stood in line, Rachelle told O that she wasn't going to Houston.

"I'm going to Ree Ree's house in Shreveport. I don't want to go too far from home. Houston is too big for me and the boys. Are you coming with us?" O looked at Naomi and Ruth with such sadness and pain in her eyes.

"I don't want to leave Louisiana either just in case Marlon comes looking for me," O said as if she were trying to convince herself.

"Baby, you have to do what is best for you and believe me when I say I understand. As for me, I'm going home. Texas is where I'm from and Texas is where I'm going to stay. You and Ruth need to stay in Louisiana and make new lives for yourselves." Naomi's eyes weld up with tears as she finally admitted to herself that her sons might be gone.

Ruth had been standing there listening to everything the women were saying. She started sobbing uncontrollably. Pictures of Leon, Marlon, Grand-mere and Marie flashed in her head. She had nothing left, but Naomi and O.

Ruth grabbed Naomi's hand and held on tight. "Mama Naomi, take me with you," Ruth was crying so hard the people in line were stopping to look at the scene. "Don't tell me to make a new life for myself. My life is with you."

Naomi grabbed both of the girls and held them close. "Ruth, I can't offer you anything in Texas. All I have are the clothes on my back and they aren't worth a dime. You are young, you can start over." Naomi was sobbing at this point.

"I will not leave you. Nothing but death could keep us apart. I need you. We need each other." Ruth's body shook. She felt like she wanted to pass out in the heat, but she had to be strong. Ruth let go of Naomi's hand so she could hug O, Rachelle and the boys. She held O the longest.

"I will find you," Ruth whispered into her best friend's ear. "A little bit of water can't keep us apart." O was crying silently and she kissed her friend on the cheek.

"Renee Broussard is my aunt's name in Shreveport and I expect you to come find me as soon as you and Mama Naomi get settled. I love you, sister." O could no longer hold her pain in as she said these last words. Ruth was truly her sister. What if she never saw her again? What if something happened to her? How would she know? So many questions ran through O's head she begin to feel dizzy.

"Next in line for Houston," the red faced police officer said as he leaned against the bus. Ruth and Naomi waved at O and her family and walked toward the bus, but the officer blocked the door.

"Sorry ladies, but we only have room for one more person on this bus," the officer said wearily.

"But we *have* to get on together!" Ruth said, with tears and panic in her voice.

Just then a round faced man with a suitcase under his arm stepped off the bus and said, "One of you can have my spot."

Everyone stopped and stared at the man in disbelief. "I can catch the next one," he said with a tired smile.

Ruth and Naomi, uncaring that they hadn't showered in days, grabbed the man and hugged him. "Thank you and God bless you, sir!" Naomi said with the biggest smile she could muster.

"He already has, ma'am, He already has."

Ruth and Naomi boarded the bus and sat in the empty seats behind the driver. Naomi offered up a little prayer. *"Most gracious Heavenly Father, we come to you today as humble as we know how. With nothing but the clothes on our backs and the heaviest of hearts. Lord, please guide us and keep us on this journey and ease some of this pain, Lord. We know you bore a much heavier burden on that cross for us and we just want to say thank you, Lord. In Jesus' name we pray......Amen."*

LOYAL

There was a chorus of amens coming from behind Naomi and Ruth's seat and even the bus driver had to say Amen on that one.

The usual five and a half hour ride from New Orleans to Houston felt more like ten. The smell on the bus from all of the unwashed bodies and baby diapers seemed unbearable at times, but spirits were higher than expected. Every now and again someone would break out in song or someone would tell their story of surviving the storm. Everyone on that bus had missing loved ones. People who didn't know each other comforted one another as they went through town after town. Finally after an eternity, the Houston skyline was visible in the night sky. People started clapping and whistling. Some sang. They all cried.

The bus unloaded everyone at the George R. Brown Convention Center in downtown Houston. As soon as the survivors got off the bus they were greeted by a line of volunteers clapping and cheering for them. Some of the volunteers hugged them. Everyone was crying. The survivors were given changes of clothing, a shower and food. The sight was very different than the heartbreaking scene at the Superdome. The facilities were clean and safe. Ruth noticed the children who rode the bus alone were kept separately from the adults and offered toys and things that all children should have.

She felt just like those children, a motherless child, until Naomi grabbed her hand and took her to some cots that had been set up for them.

"Child, you need to rest. Lay down here until I come back. I am going to call my sister to come pick us up," Naomi looked weary as she talked, but she also looked determined.

I guess I will close my eyes for just a minute. Ruth thought as she fluffed the makeshift pillow on the cot. She was clean and fed. Two things she hadn't been in days. As she drifted off she saw Leon's face in her dreams. *I love you, Leon Michael Johnson.* When Ruth opened her eyes again, Naomi was standing over her rubbing her hair.

"Baby, did you have a bad dream?"

Ruth's pillow was soaking wet and her head was hurting.

"You were yelling and crying," Naomi said. "They were about to call the doctor for you. Here, get up and take a sip of water."

Ruth's mouth was parched. She had been dreaming about Leon and Marlon. She was in a boat and she could see them in the water, but the harder she paddled toward them, the farther away they seemed to be.

"Oh, Mama Naomi!" Ruth cried. She laid her head in Naomi's lap and wept.

"Baby, calm down. My sister, Juanita, will be here in a few minutes to take us to her house. Just rest now, baby." Naomi always did know how to make Ruth feel better.

CHAPTER 8

The drive to Juanita's house was a quiet one. Naomi and Ruth sat in the backseat while Juanita and her husband rode up front. Ruth took in all the lights of Houston as they rode up I-45. So many signs and cars. New Orleans was full of the same things, but Ruth guessed that it all seemed so foreign to her because she had never been to Houston before. People drove so fast. Ruth hated fast. She wished she could slow down her life that now seemed to be spinning out of control like a top. Just a week ago she was a newlywed and today she was a widow. *Widow?* Did she just say that? There was no proof that Leon and Marlon were dead. *DEAD?* All of these horrible words kept coming to mind. She scooted closer to Naomi as they rode up the highway.

When Ruth opened her eyes next, she panicked. Where was she? Whose clothes was she wearing? She looked to her right and saw

Naomi sleeping peacefully next to her in the bed and it all came flooding back. She looked at the clock on the nightstand and it said 6 p.m. How long had they been asleep? She didn't remember what time they got in the night before. She didn't remember much of anything nor did she want to. She felt like she was trapped in a nightmare. Ruth lay back down in the bed and pulled the covers over her head. When she woke up again it was morning.

Auntie Nita, as she was affectionately called by her nieces and nephews, had gone shopping for the two ladies while they slept. They had fresh clothes all the way down to the underwear.

"Juanita has always been a shopper," Naomi said when she came out of the bathroom. Ruth was amazed. When she and Naomi got dressed they headed downstairs to the kitchen where Naomi's entire family was gathered. Some of Eli's family was there as well. There were hugs, tears, reunions and introductions.

After everyone calmed down and dried their eyes, Juanita served a huge breakfast. Naomi and Ruth ate like they had never eaten before. Everyone watched in amazement. When Ruth looked up from her plate and noticed everyone staring she turned three shades of red.

"I'm sorry. It's just that we haven't eaten real food in days," Ruth said as she put the last forkful of grits in her mouth.

Naomi was right behind her with the last bite of biscuit and gravy. They both got up to clean the table and were politely shooed out of the kitchen. Naomi worked her way around the room talking to her relatives and sharing their ordeal. Ruth sat on the bottom step of the stairwell and watched everyone. They were all so loving and concerned about her and Naomi. Most of them didn't even know Ruth, but they treated her like one of their own.

"You're pretty," said a shy five year old that had been eyeing Ruth since she sat down at the dining room table.

"Thank you and so are you," Ruth said as she smiled at the little girl. "What is your name, cher?"

"My name is Zamir and you talk funny," the little girl said.

"I do?" Ruth asked in a singsong voice.

"Yep and my mama says to be nice to you because you were down there in all that dirty water in New 'Leans." Zamir was feeling confident with her newfound friend. "My mama also said that cousins

- 57 -

Marlon and Leon are dead and that you are all by yourself here. Is that true?"

"Well, cher, if your mama said it then it must be true," Ruth was ready for the little girl to go play because she had just struck a nerve.

Just then the little girl's mother came over to see what the conversation was about.

"Hi, I'm Rita, Juanita's daughter and Zamir's mom. Is she over here talking you to death?"

As soon as the word *DEATH* came out of her mouth Rita lost her color. "Baby, I'm sorry. I didn't mean to say death, I mean, I didn't....oh shoot!"

"It's ok, Rita. You don't have to walk on eggshells around me," Ruth said as she got up off the step. Rita reached over and gave Ruth a big hug.

"If you need anything you call me, ok cuz?" Rita said.

"Ok, cuz." Ruth squeezed a little harder.

Eli's family was just as warm. She couldn't help but notice the striking resemblance to Leon and Marlon all of them had. She couldn't help but think about what her own children would have looked like had she and Leon had some. Sitting back down on the steps, she wiped the

tears that started to pool in her eyes. Just then Naomi walked up to her

and gently took her by the arm. They walked toward the back door in

the kitchen and out onto the vast patio attached to Juanita's house.

They sat down on the swinging bench and Naomi started swinging while

Ruth laid her head on her shoulder. They both silently wept.

LOYAL

CHAPTER 9

Every news channel in Houston was broadcasting pictures of the damage of Hurricane Katrina. Some even called it Killer Katrina.

People of New Orleans and around the world were angry. Some were calling for the impeachment of the president. Ray Nagin, the mayor of New Orleans made his feelings known every chance he got. There were pictures of people wading through chest high water. There were people trapped on highway bridges. There was trash everywhere. The Superdome, the levies and the 9th ward were constantly displayed on the television screen. Ruth flicked through every channel she could hoping she would catch a glimpse of someone familiar. All she saw was devastation.

Houston's Fox News channel was in their old neighborhood, but they never showed Naomi's house. They did however show the house that Simeon, the little boy that called Marlon and Leon that fateful night, lived in. It had been totally covered with water. Ruth sat closer to the TV. She looked past Isiah Carey, the anchorman in the boat, and focused hard on the scene behind him. She looked at the vehicle that was turned on its side in front of the house. She froze. She wanted to run, but she couldn't make her body move. Then she heard a scream. It was one of those blood curdling screams you hear in the horror movies when someone knows their time has come. She couldn't figure out who was screaming, but as she saw Naomi's panic stricken face standing in front of her she realized that it was her own voice. Everything went black.

Ruth woke up in a room with light streaming through the windows and medical equipment beeping. There was an IV attached to her arm.

She quickly sat up in the bed and looked around. Naomi was sleeping on a cot next to her bed. The heart monitor machine was beeping uncontrollably and that signaled a nurse to come into the room.

"Well, look who's awake," the nurse said in a pleasant voice. "How are you feeling, Mrs. Johnson?" the nurse's entrance woke Naomi.

"Child, you scared me!" Naomi exclaimed as she jumped up to embrace Ruth.

"What happened? Where are we?" Ruth asked Naomi with a look of alarm.

"Baby, we are at Willowbrook Methodist Hospital. You passed out yesterday after seeing something on TV. What did you see, Ruth?"

Ruth lay back in the bed and turned her head away from Naomi. It was all coming back to her now.

The nurse was checking her IV bag and pushing buttons on the beeping machine.

"I saw Leon's truck in front of Simeon's house. It was turned over on its side and looked like it had been under water." She turned her head to see Naomi sit down on the cot.

"Are you sure, Ruth?" Naomi asked with a quivering voice.

"Yes, ma'am. I saw the Xavier sticker on the back window." Ruth was sobbing uncontrollably now. The nurse tried to calm her, but there was no consoling her.

The past week had taken its toll on her poor body and mind. All she thought about night and day was her grandmother, her mother,

Leon and O. She hadn't been eating and she had been throwing up what she did eat. She felt terrible.

The nurse had walked out of the room and was now coming in with a syringe. As she started to inject the fluid into Ruth's IV she explained that she was giving Ruth something to calm her down and make her feel better.

"Don't worry, dear, it won't hurt the baby."

As Ruth drifted off she tried to reach out to the nurse to ask her what she meant when she said it wouldn't hurt the baby. *Baby? What baby?* Ruth thought as she closed her eyes.

Ruth woke up to the same sunny hospital room. This time it was Auntie Nita in a chair near her bed. She woke up groggy and felt the need to vomit. She looked around in a panic and reading her mind, Auntie Nita handed her the bed pan.

"How you feelin', honey? You look better. You got some color in those pretty cheeks again." Auntie Nita handed Ruth a napkin. "And to top it all off you got that horrible morning sickness!"

Ruth put the napkin on the table and looked at Auntie Nita.

"M...M...Morning sickness?" Ruth stammered.

"Yes, honey!" Auntie Nita was practically beaming. "We gonna have a little Leon or Leonetta running around here in about seven months!"

As Auntie Nita finished this last sentence she realized that she may have spoken out of turn by the look on Ruth's face. "Baby, you didn't know?"

Ruth had no words. All she could do was shake her head from side to side.

CHAPTER 10

After a week in the hospital, Ruth was released and recuperating at Auntie Nita's house. She was still reeling from the news of being pregnant on top of the loss of her husband, grandmother and mother. She was glad she had Mama Naomi, but she needed her sister, O. She logged on to the internet and started looking for Renee Broussards in Shreveport, Louisiana. There were none in the city, but she found 4 in the surrounding areas. She started with the first Renee Broussard.

"Hello, my name is Ruth Johnson and I am looking for my sister in law, Opal Johnson. She is staying with her aunt, Renee Broussard, because of the hurricane," Ruth took a breath after running the sentence through because of nerves.

"Baby, there's no one here by that name. I'm sorry. I hope you find her." The voice was kind and sympathetic on the other end of the line.

"Thank you, ma'am," Ruth said with a sad tone. She hung up the phone and tried the next two numbers. One was disconnected and the next was not a Broussard residence at all. With a heavy heart she dialed the final number.

"Lord, please," she said in a whisper as the phone rang.

"Hello," said the husky voice on the other end.

"Hello, my name is Ruth Johnson and I...."

"Opal's Ruth Johnson?" the husky voice asked excitedly.

"Why, yes it is...how did you...," Ruth was cut off again by the husky voice.

"Yes, indeed! Hold on, honey baby....O!!!!! Opal Grace Johnson!!!! Come get this phone, girl! I got a surprise for you!!!" the husky voice said in a frenzy.

Ruth had goose bumps on her arms as the next voice she heard was O's.

"Ruth!" O screamed into the phone.

"Yes, it's me, O!" Ruth cried into the phone. "I miss you! I need you! I'm pregnant!"

Ruth's eyes and nose were running and she didn't care. She was talking to her best friend in the whole world and at that point in time that is all she needed.

O was crying on the other line and if anyone was watching the two of them they probably were shaking their heads. Between the squeaks and squeals of the two women, Ruth was able to tell O about their harrowing trip to Houston and about her hospital stay. She also explained how she found out that she was going to have a baby. Leon's baby.

O kept reassuring her friend that everything was going to work out for the good and not to worry. O explained how she and her family made it to Shreveport. Aunt Renee's house was full to the brim with other family members who'd escaped the storm. O, Rachelle and the boys were staying at another aunt's house and just happened to be visiting when Ruth called.

"Cher, this was nothing, but God! You are all I talk about up here. I was going crazy not knowing what happened to you and Mama Naomi. I'm so glad you called me," O said sniffing.

LOYAL

"I am too, O," Ruth said, wiping her tear stained face. They had been on the phone for an hour and a half. They exchanged phone numbers. "I love you, cher, and I am going to call you every week," Ruth told O.

"Not if I call you first, little mama!" O said teasingly.

This made Ruth smile as she touched her stomach. She couldn't think of the last time she smiled. Had it really been that long?

CHAPTER 11

Not again! Hurricane Rita was in the Gulf of Mexico and it looked like it was going to hit Louisiana *and* Texas this time. Why was this happening? No one was taking any chances. The news showed all of the interstates heading out of Houston were jam packed with cars. People were able to get out on the highway and walk around.

The family was trying to figure out if they wanted to stay or try to leave. They knew that meant getting stuck in all that traffic. Most of Naomi's family lived in North Houston, far away from where the hurricane was reported to strike. Naomi and Ruth wanted to leave. They had memories of Hurricane Katrina and they didn't want to go through that it again ever in their lives. Ruth and Naomi went upstairs to pray in their room. *"Lord, show us your will."*

Houston's Mayor, Bill White, was now on the news telling everyone to stay in place if they weren't in the areas zoned to be dangerous. The storm seemed to be changing direction. This announcement made everyone feel safe enough to stay since they weren't in any immediate danger. There were still things to be done like boarding up the windows and securing the house. The tension in the air was like static electricity, but everyone had a job to do and they did it.

Ruth started feeling pains in her stomach the night of the storm. She just chalked it up to nerves and continued on with her daily routines.

She and Naomi registered with the Red Cross and FEMA after the storm. The lines were long and people's tempers were really short. Several times the women started to give up, but they knew this had to be done. Auntie Nita's hospitality was exceptional, but it was a bit crowded and they knew they would need their own space with a baby coming.

Naomi was excited about the baby. She even secretly picked out names for the baby. If it was a boy, she thought the baby should be called Leon Eli Johnson for his daddy and granddaddy. If it was a girl, she liked the name Leona Elizabeth Johnson. She thought these were strong, important names. She smiled every time she thought about being a grandma or "Gram Crackers" which is what she wanted to be called by her grandchildren.

Ruth and Naomi qualified for a three bedroom apartment, but they turned it down because Naomi and Eli had the foresight not sell their home when they left to New Orleans. The renters they had were not going to renew their lease so Ruth and Naomi could move in at the beginning of the month. FEMA was going to pay for their utilities and give them money to live off of until they got on their feet. Things were starting to fall into place.

The next thing to do was find a job. With Naomi's disability because of her leg and Ruth being two months pregnant, prospects weren't looking very good. The two stayed in constant prayer.

CHAPTER 12

The city of Houston was very gracious to its new found residents. Churches, car dealerships and furniture stores were giving in droves to make sure the hurricane victims were comfortable. Ruth and Naomi were able to furnish their whole house with donations and things they were able to purchase with their FEMA money. They even decorated the nursery. Since they didn't know the sex of the baby they used neutral colors.

"I've always loved this color green. It's always been so soothing to me," Ruth said about the sage green on the walls.

The little animal stickers on the walls made her smile. The room was just like she'd always pictured her baby's nursery to be. The house was starting to feel like home. Every now and again they were able to locate a friend or loved one through Red Cross. The phone lines were starting to work in Louisiana. It seemed as if the sun was starting to shine again.

There was also a lot of fraud, crime and dishonesty throughout the city of Houston. Houstonians and other cities were starting to get a negative outlook when it came to people from New Orleans. A few people were ruining it for everyone. The crime rate went up and people were scared. Ruth started to notice that people acted differently toward her. She even overheard some people saying they wished that all the people from New Orleans would go back to Louisiana.

This hurt her, but she couldn't blame them for how they felt. She was scared, too. Going to the store at night alone was out of the question and they always made sure their doors and windows were locked at all times.

CHAPTER 13

About a month after Ruth and Naomi got settled into the house; Ruth started to feel an excruciating pain in her lower back. The pain eventually moved to her stomach and Naomi decided to call an ambulance. By the time the EMTs got to there, Ruth had started hemorrhaging. She knew what was happening. She was losing the baby. Hers and Leon's baby. She wept silently. By the time they made it to Willowbrook Hospital emergency room, there was no heartbeat from the baby.

Naomi was devastated. She felt like this baby was her one last connection to her boys and her husband. She called her sisters while Ruth was in the operating room. Once they got there everyone immediately went down in prayer.

"*Dear Heavenly Father, Let thy will be done. Please spare our Ruth and keep her strong, Lord,*" Naomi cried.

Kay Jay Smith

"Lord Jesus, we know you died on the cross in order to save us from our sins. You also came here to show us that there is nothing we can't bear without you. We need you now, Lord," prayed Auntie Nita as she held a shaking Naomi.

Just then, the doctor came out of the operating room.

"We couldn't save the baby, but mom is going to be just fine," he said matter of factly. "She is going to need a lot of emotional support as well. Where is the father?"

This question sent Naomi over the edge as Aunt Lynn explained the family history to the doctor. His face said that he wished he could take back the last question.

"My condolences, Mrs. Johnson," the doctor said to Naomi.

"God's will. God's will," was all she could muster.

CHAPTER 14

Naomi also called O. O jumped in a car as soon as she hung up with Naomi and was on her way to Houston. It would take four and a half hours to get there, but the way O drove would get her there an hour sooner. All the way there she prayed for her friend. She prayed for her family. She prayed for herself. She didn't stop praying all the way to Houston. That's probably what kept her from getting a ticket because she did eighty mph all the way there.

As she walked to the information desk she steadied herself. She hadn't seen her friend in months and now she was here at a time when she needed her more than ever. She stopped in the gift shop and brought her a balloon that said 'I love you' and some flowers. That's the best she could do. Nothing else seemed to fit.

Walking into room 1209, she first laid eyes on Mama Naomi. Just as Naomi started to say something, O quickly put her finger to her lips. She pushed the door open further and there was her best friend lying in the bed looking like she had the weight of the world on her shoulders. Ruth stopped staring at the TV as O walked to her bedside. They both started crying. O sat on the side of the bed and held Ruth in her arms. O felt all of Ruth's sorrow as if it were her own.

Naomi sat where she was and silently cried. She knew the bond between the two girls was much deeper than she would ever know.

"How did you know?" Ruth asked with a sniffle.

"Mama Naomi called me," O said trying to straighten her ruffled clothing and smooth Ruth's hair. "Cher, you need to comb your hair. This ain't cute! Yes, indeed."

They all laughed out loud. Only O knew how to make Ruth laugh at a time like that.

"I know. Mama Naomi was trying to smooth it down with some spit earlier," Ruth laughed holding her side.

"I did not! It was water," the elder woman laughed.

They hadn't laughed like this since before Hurricane Katrina. Those times seemed so far away, sitting around Naomi's dinner table on Sundays with Marlon and Leon. They were all thinking the same thing, but neither wanted to bring down the joy in the room. It felt good to let loose.

"How long are you here for, O?" Ruth asked.

"As long as you need me, cher," O said standing up to go find a place for the flowers and balloons she dropped when she came in the room.

"She can stay in the baby's roo...," Naomi stopped short of finishing the sentence.

"It's ok, Mama Naomi. I'm going to have to deal with it sooner or later," Ruth said trying not to make eye contact with either of them.

"Mama Naomi, why don't you take O to the house and let her get situated."

"Ok, baby. It sure is good to see the two of you together again. It does my heart good," Naomi said as she bent down to hug Ruth. She playfully licked her fingers and pretended to smooth Ruth's hair.

"You see, O! Did you see that?" They were all laughing again.

CHAPTER 15

"I don't know how much more that girl can take, O. She's been through a lot these past few months," Naomi said with a sigh as they walked out of the hospital through the sliding glass doors.

"We all have, but we know where our help comes from," O said as she scanned the parking lot for her car. "Ruth is a strong girl."

"Follow me to the house," Naomi said.

Once the women got home they started taking down the baby things and storing them in the closet. They left the twin bed and the rocking chair. They thought it might make things a little easier for Ruth when she came home. Naomi told O about the names she had secretly chosen for the baby. Both women prayed for Ruth and went to sleep.

The next morning Naomi got up and made a big breakfast for O. She hadn't had time to catch up with what was going on in O's life.

LOYAL

In Shreveport, O lived in an apartment near her mother and brothers. She'd gotten a job almost immediately. She bought a small car with her FEMA money and was slowly trying to put her life back together. Her family eventually wanted to move back to New Orleans, but all of the political red tape seemed to be making it hard to do. The two women laughed about old times. They cried about old times. There was so much to talk about. They would have talked all day if the phone hadn't rung.

"Uh, is somebody going to come and get me?" laughed Ruth.

"Sure. Would you like us to bring the limo or the Bentley?" O said in her best British accent.

"I'll just take whatever *you're* driving," Ruth laughed even harder.

"Yes, ma'am, Miss Daisy," O said in her best Morgan Freeman voice.

After picking up Ruth and her five hundred flowers and balloons from the hospital, the three women headed back to the house. Once Ruth made it into the house all she wanted to do was lay down. She didn't want to walk pass the baby's room so she lay on the couch in the living room downstairs. O and Naomi finished unloading the car. They all found a spot to just relax. It had been a hectic few days.

"O, how long will they let you stay gone from your job?" Ruth asked. She really didn't want to know because she didn't want her friend to leave, but she also didn't want to jeopardize her job.

"I asked for a week off. I told them my sister was in the hospital in Houston and they were more than understanding," O said. "I will head out on Sunday afternoon so I can be bright eyed and bushy tailed for Monday."

"Baby, what kind of work do you do? Naomi asked O.

"Since I got an Associate's in Marketing, I used it to work for a company called Gremillion and Pou. We do advertisements for a lot of the big casinos and the City of Shreveport, as well as a few other businesses," O said.

"That's good that God blessed you with that job," Ruth said with a sigh. "I guess I will get out there next week and start pounding the pavement since I'm not pregnant anymore." She had a sad faraway look in her eye.

"Well, who wants some chocolate cake?" Naomi said abruptly. "I've been thinking about this chocolate cake all day!"

"I'll take a piece, Mama Naomi. Here, let me get it," O said, catching on to what Naomi was doing. "Ruth, you want some?"

"I think I want to have a little memorial service for the baby. Even though they didn't recognize him as a baby, I did," Ruth said.

It was a boy? Naomi asked.

"Yes, Leon Eli Johnson was a boy," Ruth said with tears in her eyes.

CHAPTER 16

Ruth and Naomi had a hard time saying goodbye to O. The week she was there was one the best weeks they had in a while. They were cooking and laughing like they used to. They reminisced about their lives in New Orleans. In a way, it was kind of cathartic. It gave the women a chance to express things that no one else would understand. They were in no way healed of all their wounds, but it didn't seem to hurt so much right then.

Weeks went by and Ruth grew stronger mentally and physically. She searched for jobs online every day. Naomi's disability kept her from working, but she pulled more than her fair share of the workload at home. She was used to taking care of people. She had done it all her life. Now it was just her and Ruth. Often, someone from Naomi or Eli's family stopped by to check on the women to make sure they didn't need anything.

LOYAL

"What happened to all those jobs they were giving away when we first got here?" Ruth asked out loud one day while sitting at the computer. "I can't find *anything* now. I have this college degree and nothing to show for it."

"Patience, baby, patience," cooed Naomi. "Something will happen in due time. We still have money in the bank and God hasn't brought us this far to leave us now."

It was mid November 2005 and the weather was starting to turn cool. They went to Goodwill and picked up some nice coats the month before. It was amazing how one man's giveaways was another man's treasure. They went there to bless someone with all the baby items they had in the house. Ruth was trying to let go of her ghosts and look to her here and now. She prayed that God would give her strength to do so.

She still thought of Leon every day. She dreamed about him often. He was her first love. She wondered if she was going to be like Naomi. Naomi said no one could fill Eli's shoes and she meant it.

CHAPTER 17

Ruth had an Associate degree in Accounting. She signed up with several staffing agencies throughout the city. In November 2006, after a year of temp assignments, one of the agencies finally landed her a temp to hire accounting manager position at a small oil and gas company not far from the house. BoJo Oil and Gas was a company that was making its way up through the ranks as a company to contend with. Their last accounting manager quit suddenly and without explanation so the HR recruiter, Cheri Gonzalez, was more than happy to see Ruth when she came in on the first day. She showed Ruth her office and gave her the tour of the building and warehouse.

Ruth noticed how everyone stared at her and thought it was probably because they had heard she was from Louisiana.

Ruth was determined to make a good impression on the company so they would have no problem hiring her when the time came. She showed up every day on time and packed her lunch to keep from leaving so she wouldn't be late getting back to the office. She noticed that most of the people were friendly, but there were a few who let it be known in not so subtle ways that they didn't care for her. One busybody in the office by the name of Sam made it his business to come and talk to Ruth at least once a week during lunch to let her in on the latest gossip and try to get any information out of her that he might be able to take back to someone else. She always treated him politely, but never commented on his gossip and never gave him too much of her own information.

All he knew was that she was from Louisiana and had moved here after the hurricane.

This morning Sam was abuzz with gossip and the gossip was about her.

"There are a few people around here that felt they should have gotten your position once Charles left," he said in a low voice, while his eyes darted the room. "They all knew Charles was stealing and wanted a piece of the action once they got his job." Ruth never lifted her eyes from her book she was reading.

"They think you are some sort of mole Mr. Johnson planted in the accounting department to tell on them."

Sam was staring at Ruth, waiting for a response, but all she did was turn her page.

"Sam," she said, never looking up from her page. "Why do you always bring me gossip even though I don't respond to you?"

"I know you are listening, but you a smart girl. You just take it in and store it," he said with a sly grin.

"Sam, do you think that I am a mole for Mr. Johnson?" Ruth asked coyly.

"Lady, I don't know what to think with y'all having the same last name and you just coming out of nowhere," Sam said as he dusted some lint off the front of his shirt.

Ruth had noticed there were some inconsistencies in the books and she also noted that a few members of the accounting staff seemed to live above their means. She never said anything. Sam was right. She had been taking it all in and storing it.

CHAPTER 18

Today, the office was all afire with the news that Mr. Johnson himself was coming back from a trip to South America. Ruth had heard about Mr. Johnson. He was a self made millionaire by the time he was thirty. He was single with no children and he had a gorgeous house in The Woodlands. Of course, she'd heard all of this from Sam, the office busybody.

"All the women in the office want him," he said as he made himself comfortable in her office. "He doesn't pay them any mind. Some of them say he's gay."

"Um, Sam? I need to know if you have the report ready that I requested this morning," Ruth said with a little frustration in her voice. She had never known a man that could gossip so much. It was taxing.

"Yes, ma'am! It's on my desk," he hopped up from the chair and ran out the door. As he did this he ran right into Mr. Johnson, who happened to be walking by.

"Excuse me, Mr. Johnson! I was just running to get something for Mrs. Johnson and...," Sam was flustered standing in front of the man whose name signed his checks every other week.

"No problem, Sam, no problem," Mr. Johnson laughed as he picked his papers up from the floor.

As Mr. Johnson stood up he said loudly, "Let's have a floor meeting, everybody."

Ruth came out of her office and moved toward the rest of the accounting department so she could get a good look at this man that had all the women swooning. As she turned around to lean against a column, she saw him. He had a familiar face. He was tall, had an athletic build and seemed very confident.

As he talked she noticed his perfectly straight white teeth and his impeccable haircut. His eyes hid behind designer frames. It was like she was seeing a man for the first time. She looked down as he turned to speak in her direction. She started to feel ashamed. Ruth hadn't noticed another man since she had been in Texas.

It was all work and no play for her. She didn't feel she had the right to. Receiving a death certificate for her dead husband still hadn't released her from her obligations as his wife. To Ruth, she was still Mrs. Leon Johnson.

Ruth was startled by the sound of clapping. What were they clapping for and why were they all looking at her? Sam came to stand beside her and whispered that Mr. Johnson had just given her an official welcome since he wasn't here when she came and wanted her to come up and say a few words.

A few words?! She wasn't prepared and her mind raced as she moved toward the front to stand next to Mr. Johnson. As she got closer, she could smell his cologne. He smelled wonderful. His crisp black suit, white shirt and baby blue tie complemented his frame. He even wore Stacey Adams. This man was no slouch.

"Uh, I'm not much of a speech maker, but I do want to thank you all for being such a great team and making me feel welcomed. We have a lot of work to do and I am confident if we all pull together we can get it done and make this year one of the most profitable on record." She looked at Mr. Johnson who seemed to be mesmerized.

Once he realized she was finished talking he said, "Thank you, Mrs. Johnson. Now for the festivities! I hope you all have made plans to come to the company's 2006 Christmas party. We went all out for you and we've booked the Ballroom of the Americas at the Hilton Americas-Houston Hotel downtown. We also negotiated excellent room rates for those of you who'd like to stay over for the night."

Everyone clapped and cheered. He spent another thirty minutes walking around talking to everyone in the department. You could tell that he was well liked and respected. Everyone waited their turn for a chance to talk to Mr. Johnson. He made them smile and he actually knew something interesting about all of them. Ruth was impressed.

Ruth made her way back to her office to continue what she was doing before the impromptu meeting. She was still trying to locate missing funds. The rumors about the last person in her position stealing did not seem so farfetched. Just as she was getting ready to wrap up what she was doing there was a knock on her open door. It was Sam and Mr. Johnson.

LOYAL

"Boss Lady, here are the reports you asked for and I wanted to formally introduce you to Mr. Johnson. Mr. Bo Johnson, this is Mrs. Ruth Johnson of New Orleans." He handed Ruth the papers and then excused himself.

"He is a handful, isn't it?" asked Mr. Johnson with a smile.

"Yes, indeed," Ruth said as she tried to tidy her desk. "Please don't mind this mess. I am trying to locate some missing money and I know it is around here somewhere."

"Hopefully it is," Mr. Johnson said, shaking his head. "Charles really messed up and now we are trying to pick up the pieces. What have you found so far?"

Ruth looked at Mr. Johnson. His once smiling face was now looking concerned.

"Well, Mr. Johnson, I am finding a lot of bogus vendors in our database. Not to mention checks that were sent to these vendors without invoices or purchase orders to back them up."

Mr. Johnson sat back in his chair and removed a handkerchief from his pocket and started cleaning his glasses. It was then that she truly saw his eyes. A beautiful, yet familiar light brown. He was handsome.

"I suspect he made up these vendors to pay himself," Mr. Johnson said. We knew something was off because the books weren't reflecting what we knew was being brought in. That's why he up and quit suddenly. I have a feeling he had some help in this department.

Ruth sat back and listened. She wasn't ready to tell all she had heard from Sam just yet, but she did want Mr. Johnson to know that he could trust her.

"Mr. Johnson, if you would give me some time I can probably get to the bottom of who was working with him if there is anyone out there. I would like to think that our little team is honest, but at this point you never know," Ruth said.

"There is only one problem," Mr. Johnson said. "You are still a temp and we can't have you working as a super sleuth for the company if you aren't an employee yet. I'm sure there is some law against that."

"I see," Ruth said with a little wind let out of her sails. She had completely forgotten that she was still a temp and had a month and a half to go in her contract before she could be hired by BoJo.

LOYAL

"I'll tell you what. Since we don't want to let you go and you are doing such a fantastic job, I am going to tell Cheri to get the ball rolling to make you a permanent fixture here at BoJo," Mr. Johnson said with a big grin.

Ruth's eyes lit up! She was hired! That meant a real salary and benefits. She was ecstatic and couldn't wait to tell Naomi. "Thank you, Mr. Johnson! You won't regret this," she said.

"I don't think I will either," he said as he shook her hand. "Are you and your husband coming to the Christmas party, Mrs. Johnson?"

Ruth was startled by the question and quickly took her hand back. Sensing he said something wrong, Mr. Johnson said, "I apologize if it seemed as if I were prying."

"No, no. There's no problem. My husband was killed in Hurricane Katrina. I just hadn't been asked that question in a while," Ruth said.

"Mrs. Johnson, I apologize for bringing back those memories. If it is any consolation, I too, lost some family in Hurricane Katrina so I can definitely sympathize with you."

"Thank you, Mr. Johnson."

"Welcome aboard and let me know if you need anything," he said as he walked out of her office.

CHAPTER 19

Ruth couldn't wait to get home that evening. She dropped all of her bags on the kitchen table and ran up to Naomi and gave her a big hug.

"Guess what?!" she squealed.

"What, baby?" Naomi said as she wiped her hands on her apron.

"I am the newest employee of BoJo Oil and Gas! Mr. Johnson hired me himself!" Ruth said like a little kid opening her favorite gift on Christmas Day!

She danced around the kitchen table holding the offer letter that HR gave her. $75,000. She had never made so much money in her life! This money would take care of her and Naomi for a long time.

"Praise God! That's wonderful, baby!" Naomi said watching the girl dance around the room. "That's a whole lot of money. What are you going to be doing?"

"I will be doing the same thing I am doing now. Mr. Johnson came in the office today and talked to me about some possible theft in the company. I gave him my opinion and he wants me to figure out what's going on. It's a big conspiracy," Ruth said, excitedly.

"Well, I'm proud of you, baby, and I want you to be careful. Those people have been there way longer than you and things could get sticky." Naomi went back to the stove where she was whipping up some seafood gumbo.

"*I know. There are already a few haters in the office and I have a feeling there will be a few more before this is all said and done.*" Ruth thought out loud as she walked to her room.

In her room, Ruth took off her leather boots and changed into some sweats. She couldn't help going over the day in her head. She had so many mixed up feelings. How was it she still thought about Leon every day, but had such a strong reaction to Mr. Johnson?

CHAPTER 20

The weeks flew by and finally the Christmas party was upon them. Ruth asked Naomi to accompany her to the party. Naomi was glad to accept. It gave her a chance to get dolled up. She couldn't remember the last time she had.

The two women spent half the day shopping for last minute accessories and going to the spa for manicures and pedicures. They laughed and talked about things like fashion and how much it had changed over the years. Most of all they relaxed.

Both of them took collective sighs when they sat in the massage chairs at the spa. As the vibrating chairs hummed and the bubble jets tickled their feet, both women sat back and listened to the soft music wafting through the speakers.

"We should have music like this playing in our 'spa'," Ruth said using her fingers as quotation marks referring to their bathroom at home.

After their hair appointments, the two women had their makeup done at the M.A.C counter in the Galleria. When Ruth was finished, Naomi stopped her and said "Ruth Johnson, you are a beautiful girl. Inside and out."

"Mama Naomi, you are going to make me mess up my face!" Ruth said fanning her eyes so tears wouldn't spill.

When the women got home they hurried to get dressed. Naomi purchased a lovely floor length black sequined evening gown with a matching bolero jacket. She found the most comfortable, but pretty pair of black satin shoes to go with her outfit. She felt like a million bucks.

"Ruth Marie Thibodaux Johnson, if you don't come on here we are going to be late!" Naomi yelled.

Just then Ruth walked down the stairs into the living room. Naomi's jaw dropped.

LOYAL

There stood Ruth in a gorgeous Mandarin red, one shoulder, floor length gown. The top portion was covered in small red jewels and the bottom portion was curve complimenting satin. Her matching red satin peep toe heels completed the ensemble. She wore her jet black hair down in 1950's inspired waves. She was breathtaking.

"Mama Naomi! You look beautiful!" Ruth gushed, with a smile as big as the Grand Canyon. "Are you ready?"

"I'm as ready as I am going to get!" Naomi said as she grabbed her digital camera. She and Ruth took turns posing for pictures. They placed the camera on the fire place mantel, set the timer and stood together for one last shot.

"Let's go."

The women were giddy as they pulled up to the valet at the Hilton Americas Hotel. It was decorated beautifully for Christmas. The inside of the hotel was just as impressive. The amber colored chandeliers hung majestically over the lobby. Christmas music was softly piping through the speakers as hundreds of people moved through the lobby. The BoJo Oil and Gas signs directed the women to the ballroom. Two attendants opened the doors to a winter wonderland. The white tented room was decorated beautifully. As the two women looked for an empty table, Sam walked up.

"Mrs. Johnson, you are stunning!" Sam said.

"Thank you!" Ruth and Naomi said at the same time. They both giggled.

"Sam, this is my mother-in-law, Naomi Johnson."

"Nice to meet you, ma'am," Sam said, with the wheels in his mind racing.

Both women could see this and Naomi figured this was the infamous Sam Ruth came home talking about daily.

"Likewise," Naomi said politely as she sat down.

"Mrs. Johnson, I love your look! It's so movie star glam with a twist," Sam said, looking at Ruth.

"Well, thank you, Sam. I like to clean up every now and again," Ruth smiled and winked at him.

Just then over Sam's shoulder, someone caught Ruth's eye. It was Mr. Johnson. He was walking toward them. Sam turned to see what grabbed Ruth's attention. He quickly moved to her side and they both greeted Mr. Johnson together.

"Well, hello everybody!" Mr. Johnson said beaming. "Mrs. Johnson, you look exquisite."

"Thank you, Mr. Johnson. You don't look too bad yourself," Ruth said as she sized him up. He wore a black wool tuxedo with a satin lapel, a crisp white shirt and a red satin bowtie. He was sharp.

"Thank you, Mrs. Johnson. And who is this lovely lady behind you?" Mr. Johnson said as Ruth moved aside to introduce Naomi.

"You know who I am, BJ Johnson!" Naomi squealed as she got up from her chair and hugged Mr. Johnson.

Ruth and Sam froze. What was going on? How did they know each other?

"Ruth, this is Eli's second cousin, Clarice's son! Is this your Mr. Johnson you've been talking about?" Naomi was looking at Ruth and Sam's faces. They looked shocked.

"Y...Y...Yes, ma'am. This is him," Ruth stammered. She felt her face turn as red as her dress. She knew Sam was eating this up. Ruth wanted to run out of the room, but she couldn't. She went to pull out her chair to sit down and Mr. Johnson or BJ pulled it out for her.

Sam had not moved or spoken since he initially greeted Mr. Johnson. He didn't want to miss a moment of this. As soon as everyone took a seat at the table, he grabbed one himself. You would have thought he was watching a movie on the big screen the way he gazed at the three people sitting in front of him.

"BJ, I haven't seen you or your mama in years. How *is* old Clarice?" Naomi said as she sat down between Ruth and BJ.

"She's good and I don't go by BJ anymore, Aunt Nay. It's Bo now, Bo Johnson," he said laughing.

"I see. You're all grown up now and expect us old folks to just change up all of a sudden." Everyone at the table gave a laugh. "I can't change like that so I hope you don't mind if an old lady still calls you BJ.

"You can call me whatever you like, Aunt Nay. Just don't call me late for dinner," Bo said with a chuckle.

The two outsiders at the table just sat there. Sam still soaking up every word and Ruth still shocked in place.

"Mrs. Johnson, I had no idea that you knew my family," Bo said to Ruth.

"Believe me, I didn't either," Ruth said in a quiet voice.

"Ruth was married to my oldest twin, Leon," Naomi said with a bit of sadness in her voice.

"I heard what happened to them, Aunt Nay, and I am so sorry. All of the Johnson's were torn up about the whole thing," Bo said matching Naomi's sadness.

"Well, baby, this is supposed to be a party, not a memorial! Where can a thirsty woman get a drink around here?" Naomi said, realizing the mood was getting a little heavy.

"There are three bars and each of them is fully stocked. The tea and water on the table are yours for the taking as well," Bo said.

"I think I will go get a cranberry spritzer, Mama Naomi. Would you like one?" Ruth asked looking for any reason to get away from the table.

"Yes, baby, bring me a glass as well, please," Naomi said.

"I will help you, Mrs. Johnson," Bo said to Ruth. Before Ruth could object he was already up and at her side.

"Sam, do you want anything?" Ruth asked, not wanting to leave him at the table alone with Mama Naomi.

"I'm good. Thanks anyway," he said with a devilish look in his eye.

As the two Johnsons walked through the crowded tables, people stopped them to say hello and to introduce family members.

Ruth knew that this walk would be fodder for the gossipmongers on Monday, but she kept her smile on and was polite.

Dear God, please make this night go quickly, she quietly prayed.

"I can't believe you are here with my Aunt Nay. This is really a small world," Bo said as they waited for their drinks. "I've known her since I was a youngster. Our families weren't that close, but we were when we needed to be."

"This is a small world," Ruth said as she stared at their reflections in the bar mirror. Her mind was racing. She couldn't figure out why she had this awkward feeling when she was around him. His presence was demanding without him saying a word and it didn't help that he looked so nice. Now she knew why he'd looked so familiar at their first meeting. He *was* family. Distant family.

"I would like for you and Aunt Nay to join me at my table. Now I won't have to sit by myself," he said with a chuckle.

"That would be lovely," she heard herself saying.

They got the drinks and headed back to the table where Sam and Naomi were sitting. Sam had switched to a chair next to Naomi. They were laughing and conversing like they'd known each other for years. Ruth could only guess what all Sam had pumped out of her.

"Alright, alright. What's so funny over here?" Ruth said jokingly.

"I was just telling Sam about your first pot of gumbo. How interesting it was," Naomi laughed.

"Nooooo, not the gumbo story, Mama Naomi," Ruth whined.

"I want to know the gumbo story," Bo said

"Please, Mama Naomi! Spare me," Ruth begged.

"Ok, ok baby, I won't tell it. Sorry, BJ. Maybe she will tell you one day."

"No, I won't," laughed Ruth. "Mama Naomi, Mr. Johnson wants us to move to his table. Do you mind?"

They all headed to the front of the ballroom near the dance floor. Sam finally realized that he'd left his date unattended while he was being nosy. When he headed back to his table his date did not look happy at all.

Dinner and dessert were served and the DJ started playing dance music. People flooded the dance floor to do the electric slide. Mama Naomi and Ruth went out on the floor. Mr. Johnson followed. The three of them made a show of their skills or lack of. When the song ended, the lights dimmed and the DJ began to play a slow song. Naomi and Ruth started off the floor when Mr. Johnson caught Ruth's hand.

"May I have this dance?" he asked.

"I haven't slow danced in a long time. I think I've forgotten how. Maybe you should ask someone else," Ruth said

"It's just like riding a bike and there is no one else." He said matter of factly.

They stepped into each other and fell right in step. He put his arms around her waist and she reached up to put her arms around his neck. He had on that wonderful smelling cologne again.

She closed her eyes and thought about what would be said at the office on Monday. She really wasn't looking forward to it, but right now she couldn't care less. It had been a long time since she was in a man's arms.

"Am I holding you too tight, Mrs. Johnson?" Bo asked softly in her ear.

"Not at all and please call me Ruth. We aren't at work," Ruth said with her eyes still closed.

"Ok, but only if you call me Bo," he replied.

"Ok, Bo."

They danced another song and then went to join Naomi. She was engaged in conversation with other guests at the table.

"You two danced so nicely. Everyone in the room was watching you," one of the guests at the table said.

"Thank you," they said in unison.

Bo pulled out Ruth's chair and sat down next to her. Feeling a bit uncomfortable about the seating arrangement, Ruth directed her attention to the others at the table.

"Well, I am going to go mingle a bit, but I will be back," Bo said as he stood up.

Ruth felt bad because she knew Bo wanted to talk to her, but she just couldn't help but think that the whole room was staring at them.

"What's the matter, baby?" Naomi asked Ruth.

"I'm just feeling a little uncomfortable being so close to Mr. Johnson, er uh, Bo in front of all the employees. I can only imagine what the word will be on Monday morning," Ruth said smoothing a napkin in front of her on the table.

"Don't fret, baby. People are gonna talk as long as you are breathing and then they are gonna talk some more when you're gone. Lighten up and have a little fun, you deserve it," Naomi reached over and lightly squeezed Ruth's hand.

"Thanks, Mama Naomi. I guess you're right," Ruth said.

CHAPTER 21

Just as Ruth suspected, all eyes were on her when she walked in the office on Monday morning. The room actually got quiet when she turned the corner. No sooner had she got the key in her office door and placed her laptop bag on the desk, did Sam come knocking.

"Hey boss lady!" he said in a sing song voice.

"Hello, Sam. How are you this morning?" She knew what was coming next.

"I'm just fine. I just wanted to tell you again how ravishing you looked in that gown on Saturday night." He was fiddling with the trinkets on her desk.

"Thank you, Sam. Is that it?" Ruth said, knowing full well that it wasn't.

"I am definitely not one to gossip, but when I got in everyone was talking about how you and Mr. Johnson danced all night and then left together." Sam glanced up at Ruth to find her staring holes into him.

Left together? Ruth knew this would happen. They all did leave the building together when Bo was nice enough to walk them to their car, but they did not leave together. Great. This was all Ruth needed at her place of work. A scandal.

"Sam, we did *not* leave together. Mr. Johnson offered to walk us to our car," Ruth said with a little agitation.

"Boss lady, that is what I said, but you know people let their minds run away with them."

"And their mouths," Ruth muttered through gritted teeth.

"Well, I am going to go back to work and try to stop this rumor mill from getting too out of hand." Sam bounced up out of his chair and trotted to the door.

"Sam," Ruth said "don't try and fix anything. Just let sleeping dogs lie."

"Yes, ma'am," Sam said in a slow southern drawl.

LOYAL

Ruth stayed in her office most of the day. She had a lot of work to catch up on since everyone had left early on Friday. Another reason was because she was hiding. Facing all of that mess out on the floor was not on the top of her agenda. Every time someone walked past her door they seemed to take a longer glance than usual.

The end of the day finally came. Just as she was packing up her belongings there was a knock on the door. It was Bo.

"Hello, Mrs. Johnson. I see you are heading out for the day," he said with a big smile.

"Yes, today has been a very busy day and I am beat," Ruth said looking past Bo at the people straining their necks to see what was going on in her office. So obvious.

Bo walked further into the office. "I was wondering if you would like to have dinner and drinks with me this evening."

"Uh, Mr. Johnson...I mean Bo...I mean...I don't know if that would be such a good idea. We wouldn't want anyone to get the wrong impression, would we?" Ruth asked nervously.

"And just what impression would that be, Ruth?" he asked with a slight grin. "I would like to take you out to get to know you a little better besides what I know about you in the office."

"I'm not sure," Ruth said hesitantly.

"I'll tell you what. I will take you and Aunt Nay out to dinner. That way if anyone sees us it won't be such a big deal. What do you say?"

"Well, I will have to call Mama Naomi of course, but I don't see anything wrong with that."

"Good, you give her a call and let me know what she says. I'll be in my office." Bo turned to walk out of the office. "I really hope you can make it, Ruth."

Ruth's head was spinning. She was very attracted to Bo. He was all that a sane woman would look for in a man. What was wrong with her? It had been a while since Leon had passed and even though she still loved him with all her heart here she was thinking about another man.

As she picked up the phone to call Naomi, her hand was shaking. When Naomi answered the phone, Ruth told her about the dinner invitation. Naomi thought it was a perfect idea and said they should meet him wherever they decided to go around 8 p.m. Ruth hung up the phone with Naomi and called Bo's office.

"Mr. Johnson's office," the voice on the other end said.

"Hi Natalie, is Mr. Johnson available?" Ruth said, trying to sound as businesslike as possible.

"Just a moment, Mrs. Johnson. I'll check."

CHAPTER 22

They decided to meet at the Grand Lux in the Galleria. A nice restaurant with a pleasant atmosphere. Soft music played in the dimly lit room. When the ladies got there, Bo was already sitting at a table.

Ruth smiled as her eyes finally rested on Bo. He helped each woman with her seat. As he stood next to Ruth his cologne wafted toward her. She inhaled deeply. This was going to be a long night.

"Did you ladies have a hard time finding the place?" Bo asked as he took his seat.

"Not at all. I've been here once or twice before," Ruth said.

"Well, I've never been here and it is simply wonderful," Naomi beamed.

Right after the waiter took their orders, Naomi's cell phone rang.

"Hey Juanita. Uh huh. Uh huh. Really? When? Now? Ok, I will be there in about thirty minutes." Naomi put her phone in her purse and started gathering her belongings.

"I'm sorry, babies," she said apologetically. "My sister needs me to come to her house while she takes a friend of hers to the hospital."

"Oh no! Is everything ok?" Ruth asked.

"I don't know. She just wanted me to come watch the grandbabies until her daughter gets home."

"Well, I will take you over there," Ruth said as she reached for her purse and coat.

"No baby. You stay here with BJ and continue this lovely dinner," Naomi said as Bo helped her out of her chair. "If you don't mind, will you bring me a doggie bag?"

"Are you sure, Mama Naomi?" Ruth asked with a little panic in her voice knowing she would be left alone with Bo.

"Yes, ma'am. I'm sure. BJ, will you see that she get home in one piece, please?"

"I sure will and I'll walk you out, Aunt Nay," Bo said. "I'll be right back, Ruth."

The pair had great conversation as they ate dinner. They laughed about things that happened in the office. They talked about the theft happening in accounting. They discussed the rumors that were circling throughout the office about them.

"When Sam said *left together* I knew it was over," Ruth giggled after she took a bite of her strawberry amaretto cake.

"Ruth, I knew it was over when I saw you in that red gown. You looked breathtaking," Bo said looking directly into Ruth's eyes.

Ruth blushed. She had been skirting around that look all night. This handsome man was flirting with her and she liked it.

"Thank you, Bo. That dress was a little more attention grabbing than I planned. Red is my favorite color," Ruth said.

"Excellent choice. I know its cold outside, but would you like to take a walk by the water wall around the corner?" Bo cautiously asked.

"Bo, I don't know. What if someone sees us?" she said quietly.

"Ruth, BoJo is my company and if anyone has a problem with whom I see they are more than welcome to bring it to me and I will tell them how I feel about them being in my business." He had paid the bill and was now standing up.

As much as her mind was screaming no her mouth said, "Ok."

"Don't forget Aunt Nay's doggie bag," Bo said with a huge smile on his face.

The Williams Water Wall was in a small park next to the Williams Tower. At night, the lights shone through the water that cascaded down from the top of the wall. The sight was splendid. Lots of couples went there at night to soak up the ambiance. They walked around the fountain and then had a seat on a nearby bench. Even though it was still considered winter in Houston the weather was unseasonably mild that evening.

"Bo, I've been doing a little research into the issues the accounting department is experiencing," Ruth said seriously.

"What have you found?" Bo asked Ruth in the same serious tone.

She took a deep breath.

"Well," she started. "I do believe that Charles was stealing, but I don't think he was alone. There is around $800,000 missing."

She paused to let Bo take in what she had just told him. She watched his face intently.

Clearing his throat, Bo said, "Charlie was with me from the beginning. I had the utmost confidence in him." He looked a little hurt. "I even had dinner with his family on several occasions."

"I traced $225,000 of the money to a couple of bogus vendors inside and outside of Houston. There was quite a bit of money being paid to these fraudulent companies every month," Ruth paused again to let Bo digest this news.

"What about the rest?" Bo inquired.

"That's the tricky part, Bo. It seems that the other $575,000 of the money was sent to an offshore account in Panama. I had the IT department dump the computer he was working on. Even though he tried to delete his activities, we were still able to back track and look at all he was doing up until the day he left."

"You've been busy," Mr. Johnson said proudly.

"Yes, I have. I also contacted our legal department to see what could be done. They want to handle the rest with you," Ruth said feeling accomplished.

"What about the fake vendors? Were we able to find out where that money is going?" Bo inquired.

"That is the other sticky part. I think this money is going to his accomplices. Sort of like hush money. Divided up three ways that would come to $75,000 a piece."

"So, we know who that went to?" asked Bo.

"Bo, I have my suspicions, but I don't want to falsely accuse someone of something they aren't guilty of," Ruth said.

"I understand and your suspicions would be safe with me," Bo quipped.

"When I first got to BoJo there were a few people who weren't very happy with the fact that they didn't get Charles' job when he left. That is usual in such a small company, but there were three people in particular who really voiced their opinions any chance they got," Ruth said. "They are also the same three that are driving cars that seem a little out of their budget." She paused.

"I can't presume to know what these three people have going on at home that might afford them these types of luxuries, but it is very suspicious to me." Ruth said cautiously.

Bo was quietly staring at the fountain. He was deep in thought.

"Tomorrow, I want a meeting with our legal team and I.T. I want you there as well. You are an important part of this investigation," Bo said without taking his eyes off the fountain.

"Ok," Ruth said quietly. "Bo, I am here for you and the company."

When Bo dropped Ruth off in front of the house, Naomi was already there. Ruth thought this was odd.

"Mama Naomi?" Ruth called as she walked in the door.

"I'm in the kitchen," Naomi yelled back.

Ruth walked into the kitchen and saw Naomi there drinking a cup of coffee.

"How was dinner, baby?" Naomi said with a slight grin, not looking up from her cup.

"There was no emergency, was there?" Ruth laughed.

"Well, sort of," Naomi said, still not looking up, blowing in the cup. "Juanita and the girls needed one more person to play cards with.

"Cards!" Ruth playfully yelled. "You had this whole thing planned from the beginning!

LOYAL

"I just thought that two young people didn't need some old lady around interrupting things. You had a good time, didn't you?"

"Yes."

"BJ was a gentleman, wasn't he?"

"Yes."

"Well then, no one was hurt and we all made it home in one piece," Naomi said jokingly. "Now, is that my doggie bag you have in your hand?"

CHAPTER 23

Tuesday morning was electric. Everyone wanted to know why Mr. Johnson, the entire legal team, the I.T. manager and Mrs. Johnson were in the big conference room.

Some of the smarter ones tried to erase the histories on their computers. The others just emailed each other gossiping about what could possibly be going on. Three particular employees got extremely nervous.

In the meeting, Ruth repeated everything she told Bo the night before. If anyone had known she and Mr. Johnson were out on a date there would have been an even bigger scandal than just a few hundred thousand dollars missing.

Mr. Barnett, the I.T. manager, picked up the phone and told one of his most trusted team members to sweep the entire accounting department's emails and transaction history.

LOYAL

The legal team advised Bo to have each one of the suspected thieves brought into separate conference rooms and questioned. The goal was to get them to admit or incriminate someone else in the taking of the money. They were never to feel that they were being held against their will and if they were able to come up with their share of the missing money no charges would be pressed against them. The bigger fish was Charles Sutton.

Cheri had three rooms set up and called each one of the three suspected employees separately. In each room, someone from the legal team sat along with an HR representative.

CHAPTER 24

Ruth headed back to her office and the whole accounting department stared at her expectantly. She gave a brief smiled and went into her office.

No sooner had she sat down did Sam darken her doorway. Before he could get a word out she said, "Not now, Sam," He turned around like a rejected child and went back to his desk

Margaret Whitmire, the Accounts Receivables supervisor, was the first employee to be called. She felt like she was in grade school again being summoned to the principal's office.

Antonia Block, an Accounts Payable clerk, was next. She was downright indignant that someone was calling her anywhere. She started to head out the front door, but quickly decided against it.

Marcus Shelby, the Accounts Payable supervisor and Antonia's in office lover, was the last to be called. He got up from his chair with as much poise as he could muster and went to the conference room he was directed to.

Complete silence enveloped the room as the others waited to see if any other names would be called. They couldn't help but notice that the three empty cubicles were in a row or the fact that they sat right in front of Charles' old office which was now Ruth's office. They also remembered that these three were the ones who ate, dressed, traveled and drove well above their means. It definitely hadn't gone unnoticed.

Mr. Barnett went back to his office after the morning meeting and reviewed the emails seized from the three suspect's computers.

"They weren't very smart," he thought to himself.

In front of him he held emails from as far back as March that year. It was plain for anyone to see who might take the time out to check their emails.

Margaret had discovered that Charles was siphoning money from the company and was sending it to an offshore account in Panama. When she confronted him with this bit of news he offered to set up a bogus vendor account so he could put money in to keep her quiet. Hush money. When Antonia set up the account and tried to cut checks to pay the suspicious looking invoices that came in she noticed that it was always for the same amount, she wondered what was going on and anonymously called the phone number on the invoice. Margaret answered. Antonia hearing Margaret's voice in stereo stepped around the cubicle wall and said, "Is this Magpie Supplies?" to which Margaret just stared at her like a deer in headlights. Marcus was brought in because of pillow talk between him and Antonia. Of course, he wanted a piece of the action. By the time Charles was done, he was paying off three of his employees to keep quiet. More hush money.

The three of them devised a plan to pressure Charles for more money or they would drop an anonymous letter in the mail foiling his whole plan for earlier retirement. Buckling under the pressure, Charles quit suddenly which was even better for the treacherous blackmailers because that meant that one of them would automatically inherit Charles' job.

None of them expected to see Mrs. Ruth Johnson show up. This ruined all their plans and definitely would put a stop to their money. Who did she think she was anyway? A barely twenty something, New Orleans crybaby washed up on the shores of Texas and busted all their bubbles. They kept their eyes on her. She was too quiet and she was always asking for records that Charles kept. Why was she being so nosy? Now they knew. It was time to pay the piper.

CHAPTER 25

Mr. Barnett called each of the legal team reps out of the conference rooms and briefed them on what his team had found. This gave them the ammunition they needed to get the information they were looking for.

Attorney Jordan was in the room with Margaret. He walked into the office with a handful of papers. He slowly placed the papers on the table and looked at her.

"Ms. Whitmire, I want to give you one more opportunity to tell me what you know without the fear of prosecution," he said calmly.

"Dear, I have no idea what you are talking about. I am the receivables supervisor. All I do is make sure the money the company receives is applied properly."

"Is that all you have to say, Ms. Whitmire?"

"It sure is."

LOYAL

"Well, Ms. Whitmire, now you can listen to what I have to say. You will be escorted out of the building by Brenda Taylor, one of our security guards. You are not to return to this building. If you do so, you will be escorted off the property by the Sheriff's office and trespassing charges will be filed. Your personal items will be boxed and mailed to you. Is all of this clear?"

"W...W...What have I done to be treated so badly by this company?" she asked breathlessly.

"You know full well what you've done and since you had the forethought to bring your purse with you, I bid you farewell. I will also advise you to retain a lawyer."

With those last words, Attorney Jordan got up and walked out of the room.

Similar scenarios happened in the other two conference rooms with Attorney Jacobi and Attorney Nelson.

All three employees vehemently denied any involvement in theft from the company. All three swore that BoJo Oil and Gas would be hearing from their lawyers. All three tried desperately to reach Charles Sutton by cell once they were in their cars, but he'd sent them to voicemail. He had no idea that his world would soon come crashing down as well.

Ruth remained in her office most of the day. She only left to use the restroom and eat lunch. This time she chose to eat outside of the office today instead of eating the meatloaf Naomi packed for her that morning. She needed to breathe.

Walking to her car in the brisk December air, she heard someone behind her calling her name. She turned to see Bo running up. She quickly scanned the parking lot to see if anyone was watching.

"You mind if I tag along?" Bo asked, not even breathing heavily from his jog.

"I was just going to grab something from Freshly Green," she said.

"Great! I love salad," Bo said smiling.

They got in Ruth's car and pulled out of the parking lot. The words Sam said to her awhile back were ringing in her ears. *They think you are some sort of mole Mr. Johnson planted in the accounting department to tell on them.*"

"You know they think I'm a mole that you planted. You know since our last names are the same and everything," Ruth said as she looked straight ahead.

She could feel Bo looking at the side of her face. She tried hard not to look uncomfortable even though she was.

"Well, you and I both know that isn't true and all will be revealed once we get our hands on Charles. Right now, we can't risk scaring him off." Bo said, still looking at her.

"Bo, why are you staring at me like that?" she asked feeling her face turn red.

"Because I think you're beautiful."

She was thankful for the stop light they had just pulled up to.

"Thank you." She said demurely.

"Look Ruth, there's no pressure here. I just want to get to know you better. I am fascinated by you. You are smart on top of beautiful. Some would consider that a complete package," Bo explained.

"Complete package, huh?" Ruth said. "More like complete baggage."

"I know that you've been through a lot in the past year. I just want you to know that I am here for you."

What could he know about what I've been through? We've never talked about my past. She thought. *Mama Naomi.*

"Have you been talking to Mama Naomi?" she asked playfully.

"Maybe."

"I see the conspiracy now," she said, like the famous French inspector.

They pulled into the Freshly Green parking lot. It wasn't crowded which was good because Ruth was hungry.

After filling their plates, they sat down at a table. The waitress came to their table for their drink order and to introduce herself.

"Hi, my name is Lynda with a Y and I'll be your server today. What can I get you to drink?" said the perky waitress.

"I'll have the raspberry tea," Ruth said

"And I'll have the same," said Bo.

"Two raspberry teas coming up," Lynda with a Y said. "You two really are a beautiful couple by the way."

"I think so too, Lynda with a Y!" Bo said with a 1000 watt smile on his face.

"Thank you," Ruth said blushing.

After Lynda walked away, Ruth reached across the table for Bo's hands and dropped her head in prayer.

Thank you for this food we are about to receive for the nourishment of our bodies, for Christ sake, Our Lord. Amen.

"That was very nice," Bo said. "I need to pray more. Heck, I need to go to church more."

"You don't have a church home?" she asked.

"Not really. My mom wants me to attend her church, but I really haven't felt that church since I was a little boy and she was making me go," Bo said with a mouthful of salad.

Ruth laughed. She pictured his mom dragging him in the church by his ear.

"What?" Bo asked, taking a sip of his tea.

"Nothing. I just pictured your mama dragging you into church by your ear." She said as the thought tickled her some more.

"That's pretty much how it went. I hated going to that old church. The deacons only knew one song or at least they all sounded the same." Bo closed his eyes. "And the smell! It always smelled like menthol. It was torture!"

"Poor baby," Ruth was wiping her eyes with her napkins. He had a sense of humor, too. Another plus.

"Where do you go to church?" he asked Ruth.

"Since we've been out here we've been attending House of Praise Church." she said and then without thinking she said, "Why don't you come with us one day and see if you like it? I can't promise there won't be a menthol smell, but the deacons know more than one song." She was giggling and wiping her eyes again with her napkin.

"I think I might take you up on that." He said looking at her.

What have I just done? She thought to herself.

On the way back to the office they discussed Charles Sutton and his band of thieves.

"What happens next?" Ruth asked

"Well, the authorities and the insurance company have been notified," Bo said taking a big breath.

"Did either of the three come clean today?"

"No and that bothers me. I would have been willing to let them off had they come clean, but sticking to the lie was their downfall. I won't tolerate a liar. I'm all about loyalty," Bo said with his chin set.

"I agree 100% about the loyalty thing," Ruth replied. "I give it and I expect it."

"That's good to know, Ruth Johnson, that's good to know," Bo said as they pulled into the parking lot at work.

CHAPTER 26

When Ruth got back to her office after lunch, there was a note stuck in the door. She looked up to see who might be watching her.

You come in here ruining people's lives. What do you think will happen to yours?

That was all that was on the computer typed note. She thought that there might be more people involved, but she wasn't quite sure. This just confirmed what she suspected all along.

She immediately picked up the phone to call Bo, but decided against it. She would sit on this for a while and watch.

Sam came to her door and she remembered that she was hard on him earlier so she thought she would let him entertain her for a moment.

"Hey, boss lady," said Sam, in his familiar sing song tone.

"Hi Sam. Come in."

"Today has been hectic to say the least, hasn't it?" he asked, searching her desk with his eyes to see what he might find.

"It sure has, but I think I might get all my work done. How about you?" Ruth asked a little amused by his actions.

"You know me, boss lady. I stay on top of mine," he said with his chest puffed out a bit.

"That you do, Sam, I must admit," she said carefully watching his face.

If she played her cards right Sam might be able to give her more information that she could use to flush out the remaining conspirators.

"Sam, you didn't happen to see anyone leave a note on my door while I was at lunch, did you?" Ruth asked gingerly.

"No, ma'am!" he answered a little too quickly. He hopped up out of his chair. "Well, I need to get back to work so I can stay on top of mine."

"You do that, Sam," Ruth said. *He knows something.*

Ruth left the office around 5:30p.m. and headed toward home. She went over the past week in her head. Missing money, fired employees, threatening letters and three meals with Bo. That was a lot for one person to digest in one week. She told herself that she would treat herself and Naomi to a spa day soon.

When Ruth got home she told Mama Naomi about the happenings of the day. Naomi seemed shocked.

"Child, I want you to be careful. A jealous or angry person isn't anything to play with," Naomi said, with noted concern.

"I was wondering something else, too," Ruth said. "How often do you talk to Bo these days?" She shot Naomi a knowing glance.

"What on earth do you mean, Ruth?" Naomi said with a sly grin. "Ok, ok, he has called me a few times to ask about you, but that's it."

"That's it, huh? I know *your* 'that's it'," Ruth said, winking at Naomi.

"Girl, stop. He really likes you and he thinks you are beautiful. What was I to do?" Naomi squealed.

"The way he looks at me makes me blush. It's like he sees straight into me," Ruth told Naomi.

"Child, that's the way a man looks at a woman when he is interested in her," Naomi said knowingly.

CHAPTER 27

For the next two weeks, Ruth stayed in her office. She hadn't received anymore letters, but she couldn't help feeling like she was being watched when she came out of her office.

The Friday before Christmas finally rolled around and the building was emptying out. Ruth had one more report to finish up and then she was out. O was coming for the week and she couldn't wait to see her best friend. Although they talked on a regular basis it was still nothing like seeing her face to face.

She hit the print button for the last time and waited for the papers to print out. She would put the report in the inter-office mail envelope and drop it off at the reception desk on her way out.

She told Bobby, the security guard, goodnight and headed out of the building. He offered to walk her to her car since it was getting dark, but she said that was ok since she was not parked far away.

As she reached her car she noticed that her front left tire was flat. She started to go back in, but decided that she would change the tire herself. After all she was in jeans and tennis shoes since it was casual Friday. She put her purse and keys in the driver's seat and popped the trunk. When she walked around to the trunk to pull out the spare and the jack she heard some rustling in the shrubbery near the car.

This made her nervous and she slammed the trunk down just in time to see a darkly clad figure walking toward her. Her first instinct was to run, but the person was standing between her and the front door. There was a flash of metal in the person's hand. It caught the light from the street lamp. She thought about the mace on her keychain, but it was in the car on the seat.

"Lord, please!" she screamed out just as the attacker lunged toward her.

Just then she heard someone call her name. It was Bo, followed by the security guard from the front desk.

"Stop!" yelled the security guard.

The would be attacker turned to run, but another security guard that patrolled the parking lot came out of nowhere and bumped the assailant with the security cart. There was a scuffle, a yelp and finally the handcuffs. As the two security guards stood the perpetrator up, Bo pulled off the dark mask. It was Sam!

Ruth was shocked. *Not Sam.* She had always been a pretty good judge of character. She never took him as the type to do harm to someone. Especially her.

The sirens in the background brought Ruth back from her thoughts. Bo walked toward her. When he reached her she collapsed in his arms. She was shaking violently.

He opened the car door for her so she could sit down. She made a mental note to never separate herself from her keys again. Bo bent down in front of Ruth by the car door.

"Are you ok, Ruth?" he asked stroking her hands.

"H…H….How did you know?" Ruth stuttered.

"Naomi told me about the letter you received. You should have told me," Bo said sternly.

"I didn't think it was anything. Just someone angry because they thought I got their friends fired," Ruth said choking back tears.

"Well, it *was* something and that something could have gotten you hurt or worse," Bo looked at her and wiped the tears that started to fall.

"Sam?" she whispered.

"I know. I'm as shocked as you are, but you never know these days," Bo said.

Just then a police officer walked over to the car and Bo stood up.

"You ok, ma'am?" asked the officer with a pen and pad in his hand.

"Yes, yes, I am," Ruth said with a fresh batch of tears welling up in her eyes.

"We have an ambulance on the way. It seems during the struggle the assailant wounded himself and one of the security guards was cut as well. We can have them take a look at you, ma'am," He said.

"I'm not hurt. I just want to go home," Ruth pleaded.

"Officer, would it be possible for Mrs. Johnson to give her statement later. I'm sure my security guards can tell you everything you need to know for right now." Bo said in a take charge tone.

"Yes, that will be fine. We will need her contact information and there will probably be an officer coming out to your house for a statement," the officer said.

"Ok," Ruth said as she looked past the officer as the EMTs arrived and put Sam in the ambulance. "Is he hurt badly?"

"I don't know, ma'am. There is a lot of blood between the two of them," the officer said as he turned to look in the direction of the ambulance.

"May I talk to him?" Ruth asked the officer.

"I don't...," The officer stopped short as Ruth broke away toward the ambulance.

Once she was at the ambulance door, she looked directly into Sam's eyes.

"Why, Sam?" Ruth asked with steeled determination.

Sam turned his head away and said, "Get away from me, you miserable….."

"That's enough, Sam." It was Bo standing behind Ruth.

"And you, Mr. I-Have-It-All. Always walking around the office showing off. I can't stand either one of you. You ran my Uncle Charles off and then replaced him with this New Orleans tramp," Sam spat venomously.

"Let's go before I have to hurt this jerk even worse," Bo said as he took Ruth's hand. "I will have a tow truck come out here and take care of your car tomorrow. I want to get you home."

Ruth followed like a little child. She had no energy. Her head was spinning.

Once in the comfort of Bo's BMW, she laid her head back on the headrest and closed her eyes. She felt Bo's hand gently wipe away some free falling tears. She didn't open her eyes until they were at her house.

He walked her to the door and as Ruth fumbled with the keys, Naomi swung the door open.

"What happened, baby?" Naomi asked excitedly.

"Oh, Mama Naomi…," Ruth wailed as she collapsed into the woman's arms.

Bo came in behind her and closed the door. Naomi started crying and both women walked to the living room. Bo spotted a box of tissue on a side table and gave it to Naomi.

"The tire was flat...*sniff*...he had a knife...*sniff*...and...and...," Ruth couldn't finish her sentence.

"The guy who wrote the letter came after her this evening. It was Sam," Bo finished for Ruth.

"Sam?!" Naomi yelled. "I knew that little jerk was someone to watch."

"Ruth, are you going to be ok? Do you need anything?" Bo asked getting up from his chair.

"Are...Are you leaving?" Ruth asked Bo. "If it hadn't been for you, I don't know what would have happened."

"Baby, you don't move. You helped my Ruth tonight. That qualifies you for dinner." Naomi smiled through her tears.

"I think that's up to Ruth, Aunt Nay." They both looked at Ruth.

"Of course he can stay. I would like that," Ruth said wiping her face. "I can only imagine how I must look right now."

"You look like a woman who's been through an ordeal and came out shining on the other end," Naomi said. "Now, run upstairs and freshen up. BJ and I will handle things down here."

Kay Jay Smith

"Yes, ma'am," Ruth said with a sad salute.

Dinner was wonderful as usual. Ruth and Bo volunteered to do the dishes.

Naomi turned the radio on in the living room and went upstairs to her room.

"Thank you," Ruth said as she concentrated on an already clean glass.

"For what? The security guards did all the hard work," Bo said with a little laugh.

"You were there for me," Ruth said looking directly at him.

"Well then, I owe you a thank you as well," Bo said drying his hands on a towel. "You found the leak in my company and you helped me plug it. You and your super sleuth abilities," he joked.

"How did you know that Sam would be there tonight?" Ruth asked.

"I didn't. I've been leaving every night after you, just to make sure you didn't have any problems," Bo said.

"Really?" Ruth asked with a bit of surprise.

"Yes, really. How do you expect me to get to know you better if something happens to you?" Bo asked as he wiped some bubbles from the dishwater on her nose.

"Good question," she said as she splashed him with the water on her fingers.

"You're gonna pay for that, you know," Bo said as he readied for battle.

"I know," she said as she dunked her hands in the sink.

CHAPTER 28

After the dishes were done, Ruth and Bo left to pick up O from the airport. Since Ruth's car was still at the office, Bo volunteered to drive her to meet her friend.

"I haven't seen my girl in a long time," Ruth said as she stared out the window. Being in the car made her remember the whole situation with Sam earlier that evening.

"Are you ok?" Bo asked, noticing her distance.

"Yes, I was just thinking about this afternoon. I could have been killed," Ruth said with a crack in her voice.

"But you weren't, Ruth. That's what's most important. I can guarantee that you won't have to deal with Sam ever again," Bo said matter of factly.

LOYAL

"I hear what you're saying, Bo, but it is going to take a minute to shake that feeling I had when I saw him tonight. I've never been so scared in my life," she said looking intently at him.

He placed his hand on her hers. "I won't let anything happen to you, Ruth. I promise."

They pulled up to Terminal B at Bush Intercontinental Airport where O was standing outside with her bags. She didn't know Bo's car so when the car pulled up in front of her with its darkly tinted windows she just stood there. Bo opened the sunroof and Ruth popped her head out.

"Are you just going to stand there or what?!" Ruth squeaked.

"Cher, I didn't know who this was riding up on me like that," O laughed as she ran around to Ruth's side of the car.

The two women hugged and talked as Bo got out and put O's bag in the trunk.

"Ruth Marie, who is your friend?" O said, eyeing Bo.

"This is my boss…I mean…my friend, Bo," Ruth stammered.

"Okay," O said confused.

"I'm Bo. Ruth and I work together and I'm a friend of the family," Bo said, shaking O's hand.

"Cher, we will talk later. I have so much to tell you," Ruth said as they all got in the car. "Mama Naomi can't wait to see you!"

"Cher, I can't believe it's been over a year since I last saw you!" O said excitedly.

"I know. It doesn't seem that long since we talk to each other all the time," Ruth said.

"I see we haven't been talking about *everything*," O teased as she poked Ruth in the shoulder from the back seat.

"Hush, cher!" Ruth blushed.

"Well, O. I am a recent addition to Ruth and Naomi's life. She's been kind of busy," Bo interjected.

"I see," O said, looking at Bo though the rearview mirror.

CHAPTER 29

It was dark when Bo pulled up to Ruth and Naomi's house and retrieved O's bag from the trunk. As the women walked to the front door, Bo called out to Ruth.

"I think I will let you ladies catch up. I am going to head out and make sure your car gets to you this evening. I will have a tow truck bring it over," Bo said as he put the bag inside the door.

"Thank you so much, Bo. For everything. I don't know what I would have done without you," Ruth reached up and hugged Bo.

Bo immediately reciprocated. He inhaled deeply as he breathed in her perfume.

She kissed him softly on the cheek.

"Thanks again, Bo.

"No problem," Bo said with a smile on his face. "By the way, Merry Christmas."

"I totally forgot about Christmas! Merry Christmas to you, too, Bo," Ruth said.

Just as Bo was about to drive away, a squad car pulled up behind him. He got out of the car and asked the officer was he there to take his and Ruth's statements.

"Yes, sir. You must be Bo Johnson," the officer said as he shined flashlight on his paperwork.

"That's me," Bo said as he followed the officer to the door.

Ruth, who'd been watching Bo from the doorway, met the two gentlemen on the step.

"Ruth, Officer Greenwood is here to take our statements about what happened today," Bo said.

"Hello, Mrs. Johnson. Sorry, I'm getting here so late, but I'm glad I caught your husband before he left. That way I can kill two birds with one stone," the officer said.

"He's not my husband," Ruth said bashfully.

"Oh, I'm sorry. I saw Johnson here for both of you and thought..." said the officer.

"That seems to be happening a lot lately," quipped Bo.

Naomi and O had done their greetings while Bo and Ruth were outside. Now they were sitting quietly in the living room while the officer talked to Bo and Ruth.

"Mrs. Johnson, had you experienced any previous harassment from Sam Feener?" the officer asked as he wrote on his notepad.

"No, it was quite the opposite. He was constantly coming into my office chatting and being friendly," Ruth said. "I never expected this of him," Ruth added.

"I see," said Officer Greenwood. "What do you think brought on the attack?"

"We found out there was some theft in my company and we believe this was retaliation for a few of the employees being let go recently," Bo said.

After an hour of answering the officer's questions, it was time to go. The ladies walked Bo and the officer out. After a chorus of Merry Christmas' and Happy Holidays, the ladies headed into the house.

"Cher, you've been busy," teased O.

"And you know this!" Ruth said.

"Great job, cute man and…" O started.

"Hold on! He is *not* my man!" Ruth tried to say firmly.

"Did I see you kiss him on the cheek earlier?" O asked playfully.

"Were y'all spying on me?" Ruth asked laughing.

"Not exactly spying, Ruth baby," Naomi laughed. "We were just making sure you were ok through the peephole."

"Uh huh!" said Ruth

"Do you like him? Who are his people? What are his intentions when it comes to you, young lady?" O asked in a father like tone.

"Yes, I like him. He is very nice and not to mention fine, but he is my boss!" Ruth said.

"Mama Naomi tells me that he is related to the family. That would make you two…kissing cousins…Ewww!" O yelled.

The women busted up with laughter at this comment. Ruth threw a pillow at O.

"We are *not* cousins, O!" Ruth yelled.

"Ok, whatever you say, cher," O said as she ducked narrowly missing being hit by another pillow.

LOYAL

The women talked all night and discussed their plans for the next day. They would go shopping for more presents and for the grocery they would need for the dishes they would take to Auntie Nita's from Christmas.

CHAPTER 30

At 9 am the next morning the doorbell rang. It was a tow truck driver with delivery receipt in one hand and a dozen roses in the other.

"Do you always deliver roses when you drop off cars?" Ruth teased.

"No ma'am. Only to pretty ladies," he teased back.

"Just a moment and let me get my purse. Do you take checks?" Ruth asked as she left the man standing at the door.

"That's ok, ma'am. Mr. Johnson already took care of it," he said.

"Really?" Ruth asked.

"Yep. Have a great day and Merry Christmas," the tow truck driver said as he walked away from the door.

"Who was that?" O asked coming down the stairs as Ruth closed the door.

"Bo had my car and these roses delivered," Ruth answered as she walked over to the beautiful arrangement. "There's a card."

Good morning, Ruth. Sorry I didn't get the car to you last night, but I hope this will do. – Bo

"Awwww! Your cousin is so sweet!" O said lightheartedly

"Don't start!" yelled Ruth.

"What? I was just saying how nice he was!" O teased.

"What's going on down here, ladies?" Naomi said as she stepped on the last stair.

"Ruth's kissing cousin had her car and some roses delivered!" O said jokingly

"They're beautiful," Naomi gasped.

"I know," Ruth said burying her nose in one of the blooms. She took two out and handed one to each of the women.

The ladies were dressed and out the door by 11 am. They went to The Woodlands Mall. The stores were decorated beautifully for Christmas and packed with last minute Christmas shoppers.

Three hours later the women were starving and decided to eat at the Rockfish Seafood Grill right outside the mall. They loaded up the car with all their bags and headed to the restaurant that was in the mall parking lot.

Ruth spotted a black 7 series BMW in the parking lot as they walked into the Rockfish. She thought it was probably someone else, but as they entered the doors there sat Bo at a table by himself. She guessed his date was in the restroom. When he looked up from the paperwork he was studying at the table he immediately saw the three women. A smile as bright as the sun spread across his face.

"Are y'all following me?" Bo asked

"Hi, baby," Naomi said as Bo stood up from his chair to kiss her cheek.

"Why don't you ladies join me?" he asked as he motioned for a waiter.

"That's ok, we don't want to impose," Ruth said.

"We aren't imposing. The man asked us to join him, Ruth Marie," O said, nudging her friend with her elbow.

The women removed their coats and followed Bo and the waiter to a bigger table.

Bo seated each woman before taking his seat.

"Such a gentleman, cher," O said nudging Ruth again

"Yes, he is," Ruth said looking at Bo. "Thank you for my car and the flowers, Bo."

"I hoped you would like them. Red is your color," Bo said looking back at her.

"You definitely have to let me pay you for the tow," Ruth said, pulling out her wallet.

"Ruth, don't insult me. I didn't mind at all," Bo said.

"Yeah, Ruth. Don't insult the man," O said with a playful look on her face.

The waiter came to take their orders and brought their drinks.

"So you are the famous, O, Aunt Nay is always talking about," Bo asked.

"Is she?" O asked looking at Naomi. "Don't believe anything she says!"

They all laughed.

"Nothing bad, baby. I just told him how close you and Ruth are," Naomi said taking a sip of her sweet tea.

"Bo and Mama Naomi talk a lot," Ruth said looking at both of them with a smile.

"How else will I find out what I want to know about you?" he said winking at her.

Just then the waiter came with their food.

"So, O, how long will you be here? Bo inquired.

"I'm here until next Friday. I want to be home for New Years Eve. We are having a big party. Y'all should come up, Ruth," O said. "You too, Bo."

"I would love to go if Ruth and Aunt Nay wouldn't mind the company," Bo said with a twinkle in his eye.

Ruth was staring intently at the Cajun shrimp pasta on her plate. She couldn't believe how things were moving so quickly with Bo without any help from her at all.

"I don't mind," Ruth heard Naomi say. "Ruth?"

She looked up from her plate to see the whole table staring at her.

"Sure, I don't mind," Ruth said.

CHAPTER 31

The women hit the grocery store before heading to the house. Tomorrow was church and dinner. As the women were preparing for bed, Naomi asked Ruth about inviting Bo to church with them.

"I didn't want my time with O to be interrupted," Ruth said

"Since when is inviting someone to church an interruption?" O asked.

"You know what I mean. I feel like I have to pay attention to both of you when he is around," Ruth whined.

"Cher, I have Mama Naomi to keep me company and you can clearly see this man wants to be in your presence," O said

"He really does, baby," Naomi added

"Fine. He can come to church tomorrow, but that's it!" Ruth insisted.

"Yes, ma'am," O and Naomi said in unison.

Ruth went to her room to call Bo. The phone rang once.

"Hello, Ruth Johnson," Bo said.

"Hi, Bo. I hope I'm not calling too late," Ruth said with her eyes squeezed shut.

"Not at all. I was just going over some paperwork," Bo said.

"I hear jazz. Are you a fan?" Ruth asked, straining to hear what song was playing.

"Am I a fan? Do birds fly? I love jazz. I played the trumpet in high school," Bo bragged.

"A trumpet player, huh?" Ruth asked, impressed.

"Yep. All 4 years of high school and some in college, too," Bo boasted.

"You will have to play for me one day," Ruth heard herself saying.

"Definitely. I'm glad we met up today, Ruth. I had a good time with you ladies," Bo said

"We had a good time as well and next time you *have* to let us pick up the tab," Ruth said.

"Ok, Ms. Independent," Bo laughed. "What are you all doing this evening?"

"We cooked for the after church dinner and wrapped Christmas presents," Ruth said, remembering why she called in the first place. "That's why I'm calling."

"What's up?" Bo asked.

"We wanted to know if you would like to go to church with us tomorrow," Ruth said with her toes curled up in her slippers.

"Sure," Bo said.

"Sure?" Ruth repeated

"Uh huh. I've been waiting on you to ask me," he said.

Ruth felt a little guilty because she remembered the conversation when she brought up the idea of church.

"Well, we are going to the 11 o'clock service. I will text you the address once we get off the phone. We would love for you to come," Ruth said.

"I'll be there. Am I invited for dinner, too?" Bo kidded.

"Yes, you are invited to dinner as well," Ruth said smiling.

"Good. I will see you tomorrow morning. Good night, Ruth Johnson," Bo said.

"Good night, Bo Johnson.

Ruth went downstairs and dropped on the couch next to O.

"Guess who's coming to dinner," Ruth said.

Naomi laughed and clapped her hands together. O grabbed her friend and rocked her.

"It's going to be ok, cher," O said. "That man sees something he wants and he is going to get it one way or another."

"I feel like everything is moving so fast. I like him, but is it supposed to go so fast?" Ruth asked.

"This man was a business owning millionaire by the time he was thirty. He obviously sees what he wants, goes after it and then gets it," Naomi said. "I don't think he knows any other way."

"I guess," Ruth said.

"Cher, don't let someone else scoop up your blessing. There are plenty women who would give their right arm to hook up with that fine man!" O said.

LOYAL

"Well, what about you, O? I don't see you hooking up with anybody," Ruth shot back.

"Um, excuse me, cher, but I do have a little something working in Shreveport. Thank you very much" O said.

"Oh really? Why are we just hearing about this little something?" Ruth laughed.

"Because as soon as I got off the plane someone had just tried to kill you and you were rolling up in a 7 series! Your life was sounding just a little bit more exciting than mine at the time," laughed O.

"Good answer!" yelled Naomi.

"Well, ok. My life has been a soap opera lately, but I plan on putting that to rest very soon, cher! That is going to be my New Year's resolution," Ruth said decisively.

CHAPTER 32

Bo was standing in front of House of Praise Church when the ladies pulled up the next morning. He looked so nice. He wore a sharp navy wool suit with a yellow tie and handkerchief.

"Good morning, beautiful ladies," Bo said with his bright smile.

"Good morning, handsome," Naomi said as she hugged him. "Ready to go get some Jesus, baby?"

"Yes, ma'am," he said looking at Ruth. "Ruth, you look wonderful as usual."

"Thank you, Bo. So do you," Ruth said as she took a program from the usher.

As they entered the sanctuary, the choir was singing 'Jesus Can Work It Out' by Curt Karr. Ruth loved this song. It reminded her every time she heard it about the times Jesus had fixed things for her.

LOYAL

They found seats near the front and sat down. Pastor Williams was walking out of the choir stand toward the pulpit.

"Good Morning, House of Praise. Let us give the choir a hand. I don't know how they do it, but they make me sound good every Sunday and yes my microphone was on!" he joked.

The congregation laughed. They all knew that Pastor Williams was not a singer, but he wanted to show his church that he would volunteer wherever he was needed.

The congregation stood up as the pastor read the passage he was going to preach on.

"Today, we are going to do things a little different, House of Praise. We all know the story of the Nativity when Jesus was born. That was a blessed event indeed and if it weren't for that day we wouldn't be able to talk about salvation. 2007 is knocking on our door. How many of us this very day would go to Heaven if the Lord came tonight?" the pastor asked the congregation.

Ruth listened intently. She enjoyed this church. When they found it, Ruth was very much at peace. She hadn't joined, but she considered it her church home.

Bo was sitting to her left. He also was listening intently.
Church and God had fallen on the backburner since his business had
taken off. He still prayed, but he found himself doing a quick prayer in
the morning or evening when he thought about it.

As the pastor was giving the benediction, he opened the doors
of the church for anyone who would like to join or give their lives to
Christ.

Ruth and Bo stood up at the same time. They looked at each
other and walked down the aisle together. The church clapped for them
as they walked to a back room with the rest of the people who made
their decision that day.

In the room, a member of the church talked and prayed with
each of them. They welcomed them to the church and gave them
information on new member classes. They also took their contact
information so someone could call them later just to see how they were
doing.

Once Ruth and Bo were done they walked out to find Naomi
and O waiting for them in the café.

"Well, look who joined the church!" Naomi said excitedly. "I'm so proud of you two."

"I don't know what came over me. I just felt something calling me," Ruth said, looking down at her bible.

"Me too," Bo said. "It was strange."

"Well, whatever it was hit both of y'all at the same time," O said smiling. "Let's go eat!"

As they all walked out of the glass doors of the church, Bo asked, "Ruth, would you like to ride with me?"

She stopped to look at Naomi and O.

"Ok," She said quietly.

On the way home the ride was quiet. Jazz played quietly in the background.

"Who is this we're listening to, Bo?" Ruth asked.

"Michael Franks," Bo answered. "My best friend, Christian and I started listening to him in high school and we've been fans every since."

"It's kind of catchy," she said as she listened to the words.

"Ruth, do I make you nervous?" Bo asked suddenly.

"To tell you the truth? Yes." she answered.

"Am I coming on too strong?" he asked.

"It's just that I only met you two months ago and I've spent a lot of time with you," she paused. "I guess it's not a bad thing, but I feel like things are moving really fast."

"Maybe I shouldn't go to Shreveport for New Years," he said slowly.

"That's not what I'm saying, Bo. I enjoy your company. It's just that I haven't been in the company of a man like this in a long time. This is all really new to me," she said softly.

"I understand and I definitely don't want to scare you away, but I really like you, Ruth. I think you are special and I am usually a good judge of character," he said.

"Thank you, Bo. I like you too," she said with a shy smile.

"I know you do," Bo said laughing as he as he patted her hand. "Poor thing."

They both laughed as Bo pulled into the driveway.

Dinner was good. The conversation was even better. Bo told them he would be spending Christmas day with his mother and siblings.

They told him they would be having dinner at Auntie Nita's house. New Year's Eve plans were made as well.

"Well, I am off for the rest of the year. Mama Naomi and I might go back to Shreveport with you when you leave, O," Ruth said.

"That's cool with me. I'm sure mama and the boys would love to spend a little more time with you," O said.

"BJ, are you still going with us?" Naomi asked as she stood up to clear the dishes from the table.

Looking at Ruth he said, "I was thinking with all that has happened at the office I probably need to stay in Houston just to keep an eye on things."

O, sensing that there was probably a discussion about this on the way home from church said, "Cher, we were looking forward to you partying with us. Weren't we, Ruth?"

Ruth stood up from the table. "Bo, you are more than welcome to come with us."

"Ok, New Year's Eve is on Sunday so I will come up on that day and leave on Monday. "Bo said with a smile.

"Sounds like a plan," O said. "Ruth Marie will give you the address."

"Yes, Ruth Marie. I will get the address from you," he said as he winked at her. "Well, ladies. It has been a pleasure. I have to go get ready to play Santa tomorrow. Thank you for dragging this heathen to church and the lovely dinner."

He stood up and walked to the door. Ruth followed and took his coat off the hook. As she helped him into his coat, a black velvet box fell out of the pocket.

Bo bent over to pick up the box and handed it to her. "Merry Christmas, Ruth Marie," he said with a twinkle in his eye.

"Bo, you didn't have to get me anything. I didn't get anything for you," Ruth said flustered.

"Don't open it until tomorrow," he said.

"Thank you, Bo," Ruth said as he opened the door. She followed him out onto the porch. It was cool outside so she wrapped her arms around herself.

Noticing that she had a little shiver, Bo walked up to her, opened his coat and wrapped her inside. Her head was lying on his chest and she breathed in his cologne.

"Thank you for letting me come over today, Ruth. I enjoy being with you and Aunt Nay," he said in between the breaths he was taking of her hair.

"No problem. We believe in saving heathens," she giggled.

They stood in that position for about two minutes in silence and then Ruth pulled away.

"Merry Christmas, Bo. I hope Santa brings you whatever you wished for," Ruth said.

"He already did," Bo said as he kissed her on her forehead and walked down the steps. "Good night, Ruth Johnson."

Smiling she said, "Good night, Bo Johnson."

CHAPTER 33

The ladies woke up earlier the next morning and went downstairs like little kids. The first gift Ruth reached for was Bo's. The other two ladies stopped opening their presents to see what Ruth would pull out of the beautiful box.

"You've got to be kidding me!" Ruth said aloud as she lifted the top. She quickly turned the box around so O and Naomi could see.

"Ruth!" yelled O. "It's beautiful."

"That is gorgeous, Ruth," Naomi said smiling. "BJ is a class act."

Ruth turned the box around so she could look at the princess cut platinum diamond bracelet lying on the black velvet lining. She couldn't believe her eyes. She had never held so many diamonds before. It had to be at least five carats. She was speechless. It was only when O snapped a picture of her was she able to speak.

"I've got to call him," she said as she jumped up to grab her cell phone. "I can't believe he did this!"

"Cher, that man isn't playing with you," O said laughing.

It was 9 a.m. so Ruth felt like Bo would be up. After the phone rang for the third time, Bo picked up.

"Merry Christmas, Ruth Johnson," he said with a smile in his voice.

"Merry Christmas, Bo Johnson," she said with an even bigger one. "What were you thinking?"

"What do you mean?" he said coyly.

"You know *exactly* what I mean!" she squeaked.

"Do you like it?" Bo asked her.

"Do I?" she asked. "It's beautiful, but it's too much. I can't accept this, Bo. I didn't get you anything!"

"Christmas is for giving, Ruth," he paused. "Just spending time with you is gift enough for me."

"Thank you, Bo. It's beautiful. I'm going to be scared to wear it anywhere. Someone might try and pop me over the head for all these diamonds," Ruth said.

"I won't let that happen," Bo said.

When she talked to Bo she felt like a teenager. She had her eyes closed tight and she had a big smile on her face. She felt silly.

"Well, I won't keep you, but I really wanted you to know that I loved my present," she said.

"Will I see you today?" Bo asked Ruth.

"Do you want to see me today?" she returned.

"You know the answer to that question," he said.

"Well, Auntie Nita is serving dinner at 3 p.m. so we are here until around 2:30 p.m.," Ruth said

"I will see you soon then," Bo said.

"Ok. I'll talk to you later. Bye bye."

Ruth went back into the living room to continue opening presents and celebrating Christmas.

"You do know what today is, don't you?" O asked as they were cleaning up wrapping paper.

"Yes, it's Christmas," laughed Ruth.

"And?" O asked.

"It would have been your second anniversary," Naomi said quietly.

A pain shot through Ruth's heart. It was sort of like a punishment for forgetting. She hadn't forgotten. She would never forget.

"I know," Ruth said. "I just try not to think about it."

"Me too, but it always seems to be there in the back of my mind," O said picking up the last piece of paper.

"You girls can't live in the past. God has a plan for everything and everyone. We can't question it," Naomi said.

"You're right, Mama Naomi," O said.

The ladies were very somber as they got ready for Christmas dinner at Aunt Juanita's.

At 1 p.m., the doorbell rang.

"I'll get it," O said walking out of the living room.

She opened the door to find Bo standing there with a big smile.

"Well, helloooo Santa!" O said loud enough for Ruth to hear.

"How are you, O?" Bo chuckled. "Merry Christmas."

Just then Ruth came around the corner. "Are you going to let him in, O?" Ruth teased.

O stepped back from the door giving Bo enough room to step inside.

All three of them stood there for a moment.

"I better finish getting ready," O said and bounced up the stairs.

"She is hilarious," Bo said

"Yeah, she is a regular comedian," Ruth laughed.

The couple walked into the living room and sat down on the couch. Bo touched Ruth's wrist which was now sporting her beautiful Christmas gift.

"It looks good on you," Bo said.

"Bo, this is really too much. I didn't get you anything," Ruth said staring at the bracelet.

"Would you stop with that? I already told you I have what I need," Bo said.

"Merry Christmas, BJ," Naomi said as she walked into the living room.

Bo stood up and kissed Naomi on the cheek. "Merry Christmas to you too, Aunt Nay," Bo said.

"Ruth's bracelet is stunning," she said.

"I think she likes it, Aunt Nay, but she keeps trying to give it back," he said smiling.

"I've taught her better, BJ," Naomi said with a laugh as she gently pinched Ruth's cheek.

"All I'm saying is that I didn't get him anything," Ruth said blushing.

"Ok, I'll tell you what. You think of something to give me for Christmas, *but* you can't buy it," Bo said.

"How fair is that?" Ruth exclaimed.

"I think it's pretty fair, don't you Aunt Nay?" Bo asked as he winked at Naomi.

"My name is Bennett and I'm not in it," Naomi said as she walked out of the living room.

Bo stood up from the couch. "Well, Ruth Johnson, I am going to head over to my mother's house," he said as he walked to the door.

Ruth followed and helped him as he put on his coat. "Bo, thank you again for the beautiful bracelet. Now, I have to go rack my brain for your gift," she said with a little laugh.

"Just remember, you can't spend any money on it," he said.

They hugged and wished each other a Merry Christmas again.

"I am going to head into the office this week to tie up some loose ends and to check on the month end progress," Bo told Ruth.

"That should be interesting. I'm sure everyone knows what happened on Friday by now," Ruth said looking down at the floor.

"They might, but that doesn't matter now. You are safe and you are with family. Sam or no one else can hurt you," Bo said taking her chin into his hand. "No worries."

"Ok," Ruth said.

"Besides you have another whole week off to let this thing die down. When you get home from Shreveport you will be ready for a new year," Bo said

"Speaking of Shreveport, are you going to join us for New Years Eve?" asked Ruth.

"That's up to you," Bo stated.

"Well, O invited you and I would like for you to come too," Ruth said.

"Then it's settled. I will be there Sunday afternoon. I usually stay at the Horseshoe in Bossier City. I will get a room there and meet up with you ladies that evening," Bo said.

"That sounds like a plan. I'm excited. A new year and a new beginning," Ruth said excitedly.

"Exactly," Bo said as he hugged Ruth once more before walking out the door. "I'll talk to you later."

"Merry Christmas, Bo," Ruth said with a warm smile.

CHAPTER 34

Christmas at Aunt Juanita's house was fun. The food and the company were excellent. Naomi insisted on showing everyone Ruth's Christmas present from Bo.

"Honey, that is beautiful! You better keep him," Auntie Nita kidded while they were alone in the kitchen.

"It's not like that with us, Auntie Nita," said Ruth quietly.

"Oh, I know, honey. I'm just teasing you, but it wouldn't hurt for you to date. You're young," Auntie Nita said as she removed a sweet potato pie from the oven.

Ruth didn't say anything as she walked out of the kitchen with the dessert plates in her hands.

LOYAL

After dinner, the family played games and sang Christmas songs. Ruth liked Christmas with this family. It was nothing like Christmas in New Orleans. It was usually just Ruth and Grand-mere'. Marie would occasionally stop by to eat and open any gifts she had under the tree. Sometimes Ruth would go to O's house and have dinner with her family. Ruth found herself reminiscing a lot lately. Sometimes the memories were good and sometimes they were bad. She never knew what it was going to be.

The ladies packed up and left around 10 p.m. and headed home. They wanted to get to bed so they could leave early for Shreveport. Ruth and Naomi decided to go back early with O so they could get a change of scenery and spend more time with Rachelle and the boys.

"Hey, is Prince Charming still coming for the party?" O inquired as they were shutting down for the night.

"I think so," Ruth said as she walked out of the restroom.

"Well, why don't you two ride up with me and ride back with him?" O asked.

"I don't know about that," Ruth said quickly.

"Are you still running from that man, cher?" O asked as she wrapped her hair in her scarf.

"I'm not running, O. I'm just taking things slow," Ruth said with a little frustration.

"That doesn't sound like a bad idea, baby," Naomi chimed in.

Ruth picked up her cell phone and took a deep breath. She wanted him to come and she definitely wouldn't mind riding home with him.

She called him and apologized for calling so late. Ruth asked if it would be ok for her and Naomi to ride home with him from Shreveport. He sounded very happy when he said yes. She thanked him, told him she would talk to him later and hung up.

She couldn't stop smiling.

LOYAL

CHAPTER 35

Rachelle and the boys were very excited to see Ruth and Naomi. There were lots of hugs and talking going on. Being with them made Ruth reminisce about the times they used to share together in New Orleans.

"I'm so glad you two came, cher," Rachelle said squeezing Ruth's hand. "You look wonderful!"

"Thank you, Ms. Rachelle. I'm trying to keep it together," she laughed, running her hands down her sides and spinning around.

"And Naomi, you are looking well," Rachelle said to Naomi.

"I'm trying to keep it together, too," Naomi said as she mocked Ruth's movements.

Everyone laughed.

"O, I love your apartment, cher," Ruth said.

"Thank you. I had to get away from mama and the boys! They were driving me crazy and blocking my action," O said as she playfully stuck her tongue out at her mother.

"That child thinks she is grown, but I will still beat that butt if I have, too," Rachelle said as she swatted at O's backside.

"Mama, I am grown! I have a job, a car, an apartment *and* a man!" O laughed as she quickly moved out of her mother's reach.

O showed Ruth and Naomi a picture of her boyfriend, David. He was very handsome. "He's a looker, cher," Ruth teased O.

"Thanks. He works offshore and won't be back until the day of the party. You can meet him then," O said.

"Ruth, O told me that you have a new beau, too," Rachelle said.

"A beau, huh?" Ruth said, pinching O on the thigh.

"His *name* is Bo, mama," O said laughing.

"I see," Rachelle said, winking. "He is coming for the party?"

"Yes ma'am," Ruth said blushing. "O invited him."

"I sure did! Why would you want to bring in the New Year without your *Bo*?" O teased as Ruth went to pinch her again.

"He's *not* my *Bo*!" Ruth yelled. "Mama Naomi, tell them!"

"My name is Bennett and I'm not in it," Naomi laughed.

The rest of the week was spent introducing Ruth and Naomi to family members. They all knew about Ruth and Naomi and made them feel at home. Everyone was excited about the New Years Eve party.

The day of the party came quickly and there were lots of preparation to be made. Since the party was on a Sunday, the ladies had their hair done by O's cousins. She also had cousins that were makeup artists. As a matter of fact she had a cousin for everything.

Around 5 p.m., Bo called Ruth on her cell phone for directions to O's house. He told her he would be there at 8 p.m. She was nervous. She hadn't talked to Bo in a few days and she didn't know what to say to him. Looking down at her bracelet, she closed her eyes and smiled.

The dress Ruth chose for the party was gorgeous. It was a strapless, tea length coral color. She complimented the dress with silver shoes, belt and handbag. She wore a diamond solitaire necklace around her neck and her gift from Bo on her wrist. Her hair was up in the front and cascaded down around her shoulders in the back. She was breathtaking.

All week she thought about what she could give Bo for a gift. That day she finally decided what she would give him. It didn't cost any money and it was very special.

The doorbell rang at 8 p.m. exactly. Everyone stopped talking and looked at Ruth. She got up from the chair and went to the door.

There he stood in his black tux. He looked very handsome. She stared at him for a few seconds before he asked could he come in.

"Come in, come in," she blushed.

Ruth introduced Bo to everyone in the room. All of O's family that was there had no problem speaking their minds and making Bo feel right at home.

"Cher, he is *fine*," Rachelle whispered to Ruth when Bo wasn't looking.

Bo offered to drive Ruth and Naomi to the party. O was going to wait for David to pick her up.

LOYAL

The party was at the Holiday Inn Downtown on Lake Street. The staff decorated the party room with black, white and silver decorations. Balloons were everywhere and party favors were on all the tables. The caterers were dressed in black and attended to every need of the guests. The DJ played all the latest songs and the light show was spectacular. There was even a huge digital clock projected on the wall that showed the time down to the second.

"O and her family really know how to throw a party," Bo leaned over and said to Ruth as they finished their dessert.

"Every New Years Eve in New Orleans was a big deal for her family so now that everyone is together in Shreveport they went all out," Ruth said over the music. "I had forgotten how much I missed this."

The DJ started playing *'Be Without You'* by Mary J. Blige. Bo asked Ruth to dance. The butterflies in her stomach fluttered as they walked to the dance floor. Swaying to the music in his arms, Ruth began to think about the past few months and how Bo had been there for her and Naomi. It was almost like he was her guardian angel. She laid her head on his chest as she listened to Mary sing her heart out. She closed her eyes and smelled his cologne. He smelled wonderful. Her thoughts raced as she listened to him hum the song.

Just then the DJ directed everyone's attention to the digital clock on the wall. It read 11:58 p.m. Everyone scrambled to get their party favors.

"10...9...8...7...6...5...4...3...2...1! Happy New Year!" Everyone shouted in unison. The DJ started playing 'Auld Lang Syne'.

Right at that moment Ruth wrapped her arms around Bo's neck and passionately kissed him.

"Merry Christmas and Happy New Year, Bo Johnson," she said as balloons and confetti fell from the ceiling around them.

Bo just stood there smiling at her. "Same to you, Ruth Johnson," he said as he bent down for another kiss. "Same to you."

- Are you an author looking to publish your work without paying an arm and a leg to do so?
- Do you have material gathering dust in a closet or in a file on your computer?

If so, look no further. **HerJourney Publishing Company, Inc.** is here to help you.

We offer affordable publishing packages while providing high quality publishing. We even have a publishing package for high school students.

Reasons to publish with HerJourney Publishing

- **Affordable Prices**
- **High Author Royalties**
- **Prompt Service**
- **Courteous Staff**

Contact us today! You won't regret it.

HerJourney Publishing Company, Inc.

Kay Jay Smith

P.O. Box 670176
Houston, TX 77267-0176
Tel: 877-648-6597 Fax: 877-655-6871
www.herjourneypublishing.com

LOYAL

Book Club Discussion Questions for LOYAL

1. Do you think Naomi ever regretted moving to New Orleans?

2. Were the Katrina survivors dealt with fairly by the government in the days following the storm? Did they receive poor treatment from their host cities?

3. After Ruth lost the baby were you secretly relieved feeling she would be free to find a new life?

4. Was Sam suspect before the attack in the parking lot?

5. Do you think Ruth's feelings for Bo were too soon?

6. Was Bo's pursuit of Ruth too forward?

7. Did Ruth and O's relationship seem stereotypical? Dark skin vs. light skin, pretty vs. plain

8. Was the Christian aspect evident in this book?

9. Were you judgmental when first introduced to O's mother, Rachel?

10. What do you think is next for Ruth and Naomi?

11. Have you found your Bo or Ruth?